THE STREET URCHIN'S CHRISTMAS LONGING

ELLA CORNISH

CHAPTER 1

*S*mall, bright eyes darted from one side of the road to the other, cautiously watching out for danger from vagabonds and thieves. Years of harsh living in London's East End had long since trained the young girl to be alert to any potential threats, the unexpected shocking her when her guard was lowered. She could never be sure when someone might appear from the alleyways to confront her and snatch what little she carried on her small defenceless body—it didn't matter that she was a young child of no more than five years.

Now, she was in the lovelier, more agreeable surroundings of the West End, but still she could not find any comfort amongst the well-dressed, pleasantly spoken upper class. To her, they were still only people, but ones who appeared to have a lot more of what she desired—warm clothes, hats and mufflers to keep them warm in the biting winter temperatures. At her tender age she had little knowledge of why they were different, but they certainly were, that much was obvious even to her young eyes.

Although she recognised that she did not face the same dangers as she did in her own neighbourhood, she still stood with just as much unease as if she was lounging in an alleyway near the ports, inhaling the stale smell of fish innards. To be sure, there was certainly a more pleasant odour amongst the passers-by of these streets. Their bodies did not smell of the stench of sweat and booze, caked in dirt and soot from untold hours in Godforsaken factories, mills and sweatshops.

The differences between these folk and those that Eloise recognised as her peers was staunch and daunting, fuelling her discomfort with each passing second. Every so often, she could hear her mother's enraged voice as she shouted out at the man standing before her.

The man appeared old—by the little girl's standards. His hair was almost fully snow white and his skin ruckled with deep wrinkles around the tight pinch of his collar. His face seemed cold, unsmiling, and unwavering to her mother's demands.

What does Mama want with 'im? Why can't we go 'ome? It's too cold out here in the street...

The temperatures had dropped to near freezing. Through her threadbare mittens and moth-eaten dress, the wind whipped up to chill her tender young skin—she had nearly outgrown her attire, but there were no funds to purchase any new clothes.

She noted the sting of her extremities, wriggling them incessantly to keep the blood flowing, lest she fall victim to frostbite. There were many little tips she had learnt from living with her mother in their tiny rented room in Mrs Bellows boarding house, tricks that small children from the West End would never bother to learn. She was fortunate that she had her mother to teach her. They were better off than a lot of folks, especially Annabelle Mullins, who lived two doors down. She had been widowed this last year and had three hungry mouths to feed. Eloise heard the baby crying constantly, morning, noon and night, but Annabelle had little sustenance to give to the bairn, being that she was lacking in any nourishment herself.

Eloise did not allow the dismal thought to overtake her and stomped her feet against the hard stone ground to keep the blood pumping. Her mother did not lie. Her mother had kept them from living in the gutters like so many other families had been forced to do over the years, eating rats and dying from consumption. Whilst it was true that they did on occasion fall upon harder times than others, Laura Miller always found a way to see them through—just as she was attempting to do at this precise moment. Eloise merely needed to be patient and wait for her mother's signal.

Mama will find us help soon enough, she thought, her vivid mossy-green eyes blinking hopefully towards her mother who still stood across the way, pleading with the finely dressed gentleman who had arrived in a sleek, black carriage. She took in the crest, wishing that she could read. Perhaps it was not a word at all but a symbol, although Eloise would not know the difference. It was a pretty design, the gold paint swirling in undulating lines, falling into a shape akin to a tree.

She turned her attention back towards her mother and the man, willing them to hurry their conversation along. From where Eloise stood, out of sight, she could see that the exchange was not going well as Laura's face was contorted, imploring the man who steadfastly refused to help.

For a second time, Eloise saw that he attempted to leave but Laura remained in place, her voice rising slightly to keep him from fleeing. Even from the distance between them, Eloise could see the flash of discontentment in his eyes, a fine line of anger forming against his already firm mouth. It seemed to Eloise, if it grew any thinner, his mouth would disappear in its entirety. It was clear that he was struggling to keep his composure in such a public place, but Laura was clearly wearing him down.

To Eloise's left, a massive carriage approached, distracting her from the view of her mother, the tall, majestic horses and buggy temporarily stealing her breath away. She had seen many carriages before but this one appeared larger and more luxurious than any she had ever known. Rarely in the East End did carriages of this sort enter the grimy, cobblestone streets. This one was pulled by not two but three handsome chestnut horses, each possessing a small white star in the middle of their foreheads. Chattering voices could be heard from within even before the vehicle pulled to a stop, mere feet from where Eloise stood, splattering her dress with muddy cold water. It did not make much of a difference. Her garment was already filthy from the walk and wash day was still some way off. No one was going to notice another few splotches of mucky brown water against the stained material —had anyone even bothered to look at the girl in the first place.

She was so captivated by the sight of the coach, she found herself moving out of the alleyway and further into the street, her gaze growing wider as the ornate doors were opened by the gloved hand of a liveried driver, revealing the family inside. Their light-hearted banter grew louder as the doors widened, each voice vying to overtake the next as they spoke on top of one another.

The mud and water from the street seeped into the tendrils of her worn shawl as it dragged along the ground, causing her tiny fingers to curl deeply against the fragile wool as four young boys poured from the interior, followed by a noble man who held his hand ready for the attractive woman to descend. She was wearing a beautiful indigo blue gown that flowed outwards from her corseted waist, whilst the man wore a fitted suit of the finest material. They were all entangled in their own thoughts and actions to notice the small, dirty urchin, gawping at their every movement. As she did whenever she was overwhelmed, she began to fuss with the edges of her shawl, watching the scene unfold in curious fascination.

"Children!" the woman called out after her offspring. "Please go in and choose one item. These items will be donated to the Lady Anne Tarrant's Hospital for Sick Children! Please don't forget!"

"Yes, Mama," the eldest agreed, turning to nod with the wisdom of his fifteen years. His two younger siblings did not seem to heed her instructions, too distracted with each other to pay much mind to anything that she said.

"One only!" she said again. "Think of the children in the hospital and choose the item with care. Remember, you will have plenty of gifts under the tree of your own, come tomorrow morning!"

Eloise's heart lurched at the thought of a prettily decorated Christmas tree with brightly wrapped gifts displayed underneath, enough to sate the desire of four wealthy children. What did it look like inside their house? Surely, they resided in one of the finer parts of town, amongst those substantial mansions with grand entrances.

I'll wager that even their 'ound gets a present, she thought with some bitterness. It defied her wildest dreams, but it did not stop Eloise from attempting the feat. In her mind's eye, she envisioned the scene on Christmas morning, so filled with toys, clothes, and sweets that walking over the floor was a task taken precariously.

If I lived in a 'ouse like that, would there be dolls and dresses for me, too? Or would there only be things for the boys?

Eloise decided she would not have minded sharing boy's clothes and toys if it meant being part of such a large and happy family.

I'd not mind sharin' with the 'ound either!

"Now quieten down and enter the shop respectfully!" the mother said in futility as the middle two children continued to ignore her pleas.

"Did you hear what Mother said?" the eldest called out as Eloise remained transfixed on his face, his handsome features startling and unexpected, bright blue eyes gazing over his younger siblings.

He was certainly attractive with his dark hair swept back from his face and an authoritative voice—as if he, himself were the father of the wayward boys. Eloise could not decide if it was his confidence or his comeliness which appealed to her more.

Instantly, his brothers perked up as if the oldest truly did have command over their actions.

"Yes?" he said again, looking to them for confirmation.

"Yes, yes," the two middle boys agreed hastily, straightening their jackets and trousers as they stood on the pavement. The last boy, a young lad of no more than seven or so spoke not a word, hanging back from the rest of the family as he waited for everyone to behave. It was only then that Eloise realised that they were all standing in front of a toy shop, Pringle's Toy Shoppe of Mayfair, to be precise—not that Eloise could read the words, having never attended a day's worth of education in her life.

The bell tinkled as the father opened the door, allowing for his gleeful brood to enter, but Eloise's attention had already shifted toward the window, paling at the glorious sights in front of her. The melancholic scent of wood and varnish touched the girl's nostrils, taking her thoughts to another time and place before, once more, she was left standing on the slushy, frozen street, peering into the gayly lit window beyond.

Intricate wooden dolls with prettily painted faces lined the front of the glass. A large, gold and white rocking horse with a mane of silver tassels sat in the centre of the display, looking magnificent and ready for any child to ride upon. Tiny nutcrackers marched in various poses. Towards the back was a large dolls house, each room filled tiny furniture, decorated with lavish furnishings.

In a small corner, neglected or discarded, sat another horse, painted in chipped brown paint, plain but for a brightly painted saddle of red. It was much too shoddy to be part of the display, possibly left there by mistake. Eloise reasoned that someone must have picked it up and placed it there when faced with a prettier, better choice, but she found the pony beguiling and could not stop staring at it from her spot on the cold street. In that moment, she would have done just about anything to have that pony as her own, to hold and cherish. The urge to touch the smooth whittled wood was insurmountable.

And decidedly ridiculous.

Tiny or not, her mother could not afford a single object in that shop, or any other premises on the Mayfair Street, and Eloise had enough sense not to ask her for it. They often did not have enough money for food to last the week. Although her mother had not specifically said so, Eloise knew that was why they had come to the West End today. The rent would soon be upon them once more and Mrs Bellows was not a patient woman when it came to late payment.

"Happy Christmas!" someone yelled drunkenly from across the roadway, drawing Eloise's attention momentarily away from the toy shop and back onto the street, where she belonged. She sighed heavily and turned to look from where the boisterous voice had come.

The inebriated man was not speaking to her but to his own neighbours who replied with a laugh and a smile, their chatter of the upcoming church service reminding her of the day.

Despite her inability to read, she was well aware of the date. It was impossible to overlook the evergreen wreaths and jaunty scarlet bows wrapped tightly against the street lamps. Signs advertising Christmas had hung for weeks all over town and although she could not actually read the words, she was able to recognise the implication when she came across the brightly coloured signs.

Today was Christmas Eve, and if all went well with the elderly gentleman, then she and her mother would be enjoying a simple meal by the small hearth in their rented room before making their way to midnight mass. It was still quite early in the day but soon the shops would close, and the shopkeepers would rush home to spend time with their beloved families.

Just like Mama and me will be together, cozy and warm, Eloise thought, hopefully. That was what she had promised, and Eloise had faith in her mother's ability to see them through yet another month of uncertainty. She could not recall exactly the previous weeks and years leading up to this moment but, somehow, her mother had managed to get them to this position and this year would be no different.

A small gust of wind snaked down her spine and she wrapped the threadbare shawl more tightly around her skinny shoulders, her eyes trailing back towards her mother. The throng of passersby had grown, blocking her vision but the handsomely dressed man still remained in view. With the fading light his face had become more distant. Once more, he tried to leave but her mother grabbed at his arm, causing his voice to rise and reach her ears.

What is she tellin' 'im te make 'im stay? Why doesn't 'e just leave 'er where she stands?

She may have been too young to understand the intricacies of class, but she certainly knew that an upperclassman would not stand for being cornered by a lowly woman under any circumstance. Her mother clearly had something of interest to keep him where he stood.

"Unhand me, woman!" the stranger cried, his voice sounding angry and indignant. His tone sent shivers down Eloise's spine and her instinct was to help her mother, but she dared not. She had given explicit instructions for her to remain out of sight and the child knew better than to contradict her mother. Yet her mother clung to the gentleman, her own voice low and unheeded as she spoke, but there was an urgency in her eyes that was palpable.

Is there somethin' I can do te 'elp? Eloise pondered as she took in the scene.

It was a daunting thought for a girl of only five years, particularly when she had no idea what it was her mother demanded of the man. She only knew that Laura had vowed that this long walk to the West End would be worthwhile and solve their troubles, for a small time, at the very least.

The bell to the store chimed again, once more flooding her nose with the nostalgic smell of wood and paint. Eloise turned, blinking in surprise to see the family filing across the threshold. How long had they been inside? It had not seemed very long, but they all carried wrapped packages in their hands, smiling happily as they marched toward the carriage. She had not realised so much time had passed already. As much as she wanted to help her mother, she could not resist staring at the family, wondering about them and their purchases.

One by one, each member of the family made their way toward the waiting carriage, the driver holding the door and accepting the items as they moved to sit inside the warm interior. The two middle boys first, still playing and arguing fiercely amongst themselves, despite several warnings by both their parents.

The eldest sighed deeply, rolling his eyes heavenward as he grumbled, the youngest child lagging behind as his family piled into the coach.

"Come along now, son," the mother called from inside as the smallest boy lingered by the door of the shop. Curiously, Eloise turned toward him, wondering what had stopped him from joining the rest of his family. To her surprise, he stared directly back at her, taking her aback. Like his oldest brother, his eyes were dark and intense but unlike the eldest sibling, his face was awkward and not handsome in the least. His ears protruded gawkily from his oval-shaped head; a buck-toothed smile peeked nervously from between his thin lips as he extended the bag in his hand. Eloise stared directly back at him, confounded. She longed to ask him what he was gawping at when he spoke up.

"Go on," he said, gesturing toward Eloise. "Take it."

Eloise froze, blinking several times.

She remained motionless, waiting, as if she expected the ground to open up beneath her feet and swallow her whole. Never had such a well-dressed young person spoken a word in her direction.

"Well, are you going to take it?" he pressed when she did not move.

"Me?" she asked dumbly. "Are ye talkin' te me?"

He nodded eagerly, his silly smile growing as she looked behind her, certain that he could not be saying anything to her. As she suspected, there was no one standing behind her, but the fact did not ease her confusion in the least.

"You need not be afraid," he offered. "Go on."

Tentatively, she inched towards him, and he met her halfway, gazing nervously toward the carriage where his mother began to disembark.

"Tommy!" his mother called out. "What are you doing, child? It is freezing and about to snow, come into the warm."

The tinge of concern in her words made Eloise's young heart flutter.

"Come along, son!" his father added, poking his head out from the door. "Jack, go fetch your brother, will you? We haven't time for this today. We need to take the toys to the hospital then be home in time for the guests to arrive."

"Hurry now," the boy insisted, pressing the package into her hand. "Open it while I'm able to watch!"

Watch what? Eloise longed to ask but her throat was dry, and nothing spilled from her sore, cracked lips.

Swallowing her wariness, Eloise opened the bag with shaking hands, convinced that she was the brunt of a cruel joke. Yet, as the packaging fell away, she found herself staring at the small wooden horse she had admired from the window, the one with the painted red saddle, standing neglected in the corner. Dubiously, she gaped at the item in her hand then back at the boy, a mist colouring her vision.

"W-what is it t-then?" she mumbled, unable to formulate her question coherently. He frowned, appearing flustered by her question.

"You were looking at it, weren't you?" he asked, cocking his head to one side. "I saw you admiring it from the window. This is the right one, isn't it? Oh, it's too late to exchange it now. Forgive me if I got it wrong."

Heat stained Eloise's cheeks but before she was able to say another word, the boy spoke again.

"I must go," he mumbled, hurrying off towards his parents. Gaping, Eloise stared after him, but he did not look back as he was herded into the carriage, his mother lecturing him about the dangers of getting too cold. She had apparently missed the interaction between them, Eloise invisible to her, as most street urchins were to those of the higher classes.

Eloise could not tear her eyes from the back of the carriage, even as it slipped away into the street beyond. She willed the back curtain to move, for the boy to peer out and offer her one last, goofy smile, but he did not. She longed to yell after him, to cry out that he had purchased the correct horse, that she loved it with all her heart, but it was too late. The boy was gone forever, never to be seen again, or so she thought.

"ENOUGH!"

Gasping, Eloise whirled around, the shout loud enough to attract the attention of everyone on the street. Even without looking, she knew from where the cry had come. The gentleman at her mother's side had finally wrenched himself free of her hold, his gloved hands held up as if to cast off her mother's spell. "I will not tell you again! If you have any sense at all, you'll be on your way and not bother me again with your petty questions and demands!"

A low murmur of disapproval rippled along the cobblestones, folks staring directly towards the shabbily dressed woman who suddenly realised she was the centre of everyone's attention. Humiliated, her mother backed away from the gentleman and dropped her head, shielding her face against the curve of her frayed, broken bonnet. Strands of dark hair, slipping from her prim bun to fall tiredly along her face, shadowed the lines that formed at the corners of her russet eyes. There was barely a brim left around the hat, but her mother continued to refer to it as her "best". Eloise didn't remind her that she did not possess another.

Reaching her daughter's side, she took Eloise's arm quickly, guiding her away from the midst of the whispers as Eloise hid the toy horse along the folds of her shawl. She did not wish to explain how she had come upon the precious gift, lest her mother insist she return it. She knew her mother's opinion on offerings from strangers, particularly from those of the male variety.

Not that Mama would believe 'ow I came by it in the first place.

She was not sure she believed it herself. Had the young, boy —this Tommy—truly used his one gift to bequeath her a present?

"Come along, lovey," her mother grumbled, shoving her gently over the street, inadvertently pushing her into a deep puddle. Eloise slipped but Laura caught her before she could fall to the ground.

"Watch yer step, girl," she muttered, righting her daughter before marching her onward. Her mother turned her head away, blinking furiously and Eloise's heart sank as she realised there were fresh tears in her eyes.

"Mama, are ye cryin'?" she asked, dumbfounded to know that grown-ups could shed tears too. Frowning, her mother wiped her face with the back of her hands and shook her head.

"Don't be daft," she continued, tugging on Eloise's arm. "We are strong lasses, aren't we Ellie? We don't cry for nothin', ye 'ear me? We're Millers, Ellie. We don't cry."

Eloise nodded and abruptly, her mother stopped, pulling her daughter into a tight unexpected embrace.

"Don't ye worry about nothin'," she told the girl, her words raspy as she clung to Eloise. "Mama will find another way te pay Mrs Bellows this week, won't she? Mama always finds a way te pay the rent, even without the 'elp of nobody else, doesn't she?"

Not for the first time, Eloise caught the timbre of a more refined tone to her words, as though she spoke roughly for the benefit of her surroundings, not because she had been raised to speak in the gruff, rough manner of the streets.

"Ellie? Did ye 'ear what I said?"

"Yes, Mama."

"Good girl, Ellie." Laura's eyes shone with emotion, a thick swallow forcing a bob down her throat. "Come along, lovey. We 'ave a long, cold walk ahead of us, yeah?"

Sniffling, she released her daughter and continued marching east, back toward their grimy one room home, but Eloise lingered behind for half a moment, her small fingers curling around the wooden treasure she had just acquired. Her eyes trailed in the direction that the carriage had long since disappeared from, a small part of her willing it to return.

Still, this Christmas would be a memorable one for her, despite trudging through the dirty, smelly, freezing streets of London Town.

CHAPTER 2

❧

CHRISTMAS EVE- THREE YEARS LATER

*I*n the near distance, church bells rang, four, five, six times as Eloise counted them in her head. She marched her feet to the rhythm of each ding, sliding her feet over the cobbles of the street until her mother stopped.

"Yer dawdlin', Ellie," she huffed, glancing back over her shoulder, readjusting the heavy hessian sack on her shoulder as she did. The gesture toppled the tin bucket from her hands which landed in a nearby snowbank, the handle of her broom jabbing into the pile thereafter. The girl grimaced at the sight of her mother in trouble, and she rushed to help her collect the fallen items. The woman groaned loudly.

"We've a walk ahead of us, girlie," she reminded her daughter. "Ye'd do better to fixate on gettin' us 'ome and not dancin' in the streets."

"I'm not dancin'," Eloise protested.

"Yer slowin' us down, that's for sure, and it's been quite a day, Ellie," her mother grumbled, her nerves frayed from countless hours of cleaning work. "Ye can't be starin' up at the 'eavens and walkin' at the same time."

Eloise did not bother to argue with her mother's assessment of where her eyes had been. In fact, she had not been looking at the gloomy, grey sky at all, one that was threatening to open up and dump yet another load of snow upon their heads that Christmas Eve. On the contrary—her eyes had been taking in the surroundings with mounting excitement as she recognised the area where they were walking. Lugging the cumbersome cleaning supplies from various establishments to public houses along the West End they had been fortunate enough to earn money over the past year as cleaners. It had proven lucrative enough to ensure that their rent was paid for the most part. The work was exhausting and unpredictable, but it was a rare occurrence that someone did not take pity upon the green-eyed girl and her weary looking but attractive mother to offer some labour, at least once a day.

It had kept them fed and housed, Mrs Bellows demands at bay with her porcine face and stubby, sweaty palms. Her mother had ambitions that by next year, they would be working in the better businesses, maybe even able to afford nicer lodgings.

"Some of them 'ouses even 'ave indoor plumbing, I 'ear," her mother informed her, pointing to a large mansion house. "Wouldn't it be nice to end up in a 'ouse like that?"

Eloise was less certain, but she did not dampen her mother's spirits. She kept her scepticism to herself.

"Ellie!" Her mother frowned. "Come along, girl!"

"I'm comin', Mama," the girl reassured her, picking up her own pail and shuffling forward, her pulse quickening as they continued up the street. There was plenty more miles to walk before they made it home, but she wanted to linger, if only for a moment, in that very spot, the memory flooding her as if a warm wave of summer air blew over her. She had seen it coming but now that it was upon her, it stole her breath again.

She still could not read the Pringles name, but the toy display was almost identical to the one she had seen three years earlier. The very same white and gold horse, with its silver tassels, sat in the window, unclaimed, the wooden dolls still smiling prettily at her, the nutcrackers continuing their march along the glass pane.

Is it the same every year...

Of course, the toys were new, the old ones having been bought over the years. She never had understood the appeal of the buck-toothed, moustached nutcrackers, donned in military uniforms which were much too bright for any army. It defied logic to her mind but it mattered little what she thought. She would never have the means to purchase these toys or any others.

Yet this display looked different, despite its similarities to the previous years and she knew why immediately. In her mind's eye, she envisioned a small, forgotten pony, pressed to the side of the glass, ignored but for the small hands of a boy with astute eyes and a lopsided smile. Eloise's heart ached at the thought of the gift, long since sold when her mother had chanced upon it, not long after Tommy had bequeathed it to her.

"No, Mama, ye can't take it!" Eloise had pleaded. "It was given te me as a gift!"

It had been the wrong answer to give.

"I don't care where it came from," Laura had declared, her eyes narrowing with suspicion. "It's worth somethin' te someone and it serves little purpose 'ere, now does it? Anyway, what've I told ye about accepting gifts from people ye don't know? Nothin' good will ever come of it, I promise ye that."

Eloise had little say in the matter, and ultimately, her mother had pawned the piece, never for the girl to lay eyes on it again. She could not be sure how much her mother had got for it, but she reckoned it could not have been much, and Eloise had almost put the horse from her mind until that moment.

"ELLIE! For God's sake!"

"I'm comin', Ma," she mumbled, picking up her pace, but as she moved, she lost her own grip on the handle of her broom, caused by a blister popping on one of her hands. She winced lightly but her mother did not appear to notice as her eyes traveled upward, a small, almost amused frown touching her lips.

"It looks like snow, don't it?"

Eloise grimaced, placing her finger in her mouth. She hoped it would not snow. She was not sure which was worse— having no money to burn coal in the grate or having coal and the thick smoke choking the air from her lungs in their poorly ventilated room. Wood was no better and just as expensive. She wondered how the wealthy managed to keep from choking and gagging with their half dozen fireplaces, one for every room of the house.

Well, that's the answer, innit? Eloise thought with some bitterness. *They 'ave the room to escape the smoke.*

"Oy, lassie!" a man called out from across the way and Eloise turned, realising that he was speaking to her mother. He stood before the very same tavern as the last drunken man had called out his Christmas greetings from, all those years earlier. Eloise was consumed by the memory, as if she had lived this very moment already. The feeling was daunting, both comfortable and unnerving.

Laura cast the man a scathing look but made no comment toward him, even as he leered at her more.

"Oy, come over here! I'll buy you a glass of port if you like!"

His tone made Eloise queasy, and she looked at her mother nervously, but she was angry rather than perturbed by his suggestion.

"Come on, girl," Laura huffed angrily. "Ye'll pay no mind te that man, or any other, if ye know what's good for ye."

She pushed her daughter onto the street, shaking her head furiously.

"Men will be yer downfall if ye allow it, Ellie, ye mark me words. They'll fill yer 'ead with promises they 'ave no intentions of keepin', that's for sure."

Eloise swallowed the question of why men would do that and what made them so different to women. She had heard this very lecture far too many times in her young life to encourage it. She did not understand what it was that men wanted from women that would make them lie and promise falsely but she did know that her own father had done as much to her mother. Many nights, the girl had lain awake, shivering against the thin, holey blankets, exhausted from a day's worth of cleaning and walking. Eloise thought about the man whom she had seen her mother confront, three

Christmases ago, right there, down that very street. Could he have been her father? There had been no others that the girl could recall over the years and the intensity of their discussion had always stuck to Eloise like treacle. It seemed more and more likely that her mother had gone to that man —that cold, grey man—begging him to acknowledge his daughter, and he had simply sent her away again.

"Fickle liars, the lot," her mother went on. "Ye'll be wise te keep yer distance and die a spinster."

"A spinster!"

"There are worse things than being without a man," she reassured her.

Like being lumbered with a daughter and no 'usband, Eloise thought sadly. She did not fault her mother for being embittered but she could not imagine a life where she might forever be alone.

"At least ye 'ave me, right, Ma?" Eloise asked softly, eyeing her mother worriedly as though she were afraid of the answer.

"Ellie, if I were te do it all over again—"

The sound of racing horse hooves stopped her mother mid-sentence, panic overtaking her face. Abruptly, she shoved her daughter out of the street as a carriage teetered by, showering them in cold, snowy water.

"That bloody fool!" her mother choked, grabbing and righting Eloise with concern etched on her face. "Are ye all right?"

Her dark eyes raked over Eloise's shaking frame, but the girl nodded.

The young driver chortled, pulling back on the reins with a laugh and a tip of his hat. He appeared to be still under twenty years, his eyes bloodshot with alcohol as he whizzed by. He waved by way of an apology, but her mother was not placated.

"Bloody idiots," her mother muttered again but that was not the end of it. Abruptly, the carriage stopped, the horses fussing at the driver's unruly handling. Her mother straightened up, her eyes narrowing.

"What does 'e want now?" she muttered.

"I don't know," Eloise replied.

"Hush up," she instructed, and Eloise did as she was told.

Her mother eyed the young man warily, extending her hand protectively toward Eloise.

"By the look of your supplies you are a cleaning woman?" the man asked, his eyes lighting up as he scanned over their supplies before resting on Laura's sceptical face. Startled by the question, Laura glanced at her daughter and nodded, her head bobbing in all directions as she tried to make sense of his rationale. The boy appeared delighted by the assertion.

"Oh, Good lord, what a blessed day!" He laughed, slapping a hand to his leg before leaping to the ground to stumble toward them in a faltering manner. He was even more inebriated than Eloise had initially thought. But for his reddened eyes and bloated face, he might have been an attractive boy, but the stench of whiskey assaulted the girl's nostrils, flipping her stomach. She turned her head away to prevent herself from growing nauseous. Eloise felt the muscles in the base of her neck stiffen as she looked uneasily at her mother, willing her to heed her own advice about the dangers of men. "Would you clean the carriage for me?"

Laura appeared baffled by the request.

"The carriage?" she echoed.

"Yes. This one, to be precise," he said, waving his hand toward the very one behind him. "I'll pay you well."

Eloise instantly regarded the interest in her mother's eyes and her heart sank. She did not like the prospect of taking on yet another job at this hour of the day, especially on Christmas Eve, nor the notion of cleaning a carriage. Plus, she was also unsure about the intoxicated young man and his drunken promises.

"It's not a chore we usually undertake," Laura informed him truthfully, but she did not refuse, much to her daughter's chagrin.

"It shouldn't take too long," the young man insisted. "As you can see, I was rather unkind to my father's vehicle today and he'll not take kindly to seeing it in this state when I return home. Truth be told, I took it without permission and I'd rather he not discover that fact. All I ask is that you give it a good wipe down, care for the mud and…"

He sniffed and snickered, craning his neck around toward the cab. It was only then that Eloise realised that others rode within.

"…and whatever is in the interior once my companions are dismissed. Oh, and the horses, of course. They'll need a good brushing, too."

"The horses…" her mother murmured, pondering the notion. Eloise was aghast.

"Mama…" Eloise squeaked but she put a stern hand on her daughter's shoulder.

"We'll require water for such a task," Laura informed him. "And we can't do it by the side of the road."

"There's plenty of land before we get to the house, with well water nearby," the young man explained. "I'll rid the carriage of the others, find a spot for you to perform your cleaning and take the carriage back unmarked."

"Mama…" Eloise murmured again but Laura ignored her daughter's upset.

"All right, we'll do it," the woman agreed. "For ten pennies."

Eloise almost laughed at the ridiculous ask, hope flooding through her. Surely, the boy would not agree to such a sum, but the young man did not flinch.

"Accepted," he agreed without hesitation, making Eloise wonder precisely how much alcohol he had consumed. "Come along, before it gets too dark. I've already been gone much too long, and my father is quick to suspicion."

He ushered the pair toward the waiting carriage, not bothering to help with their supplies.

Surely, she should ask for the money first. What if he doesn't pay us and we're stranded without means to get 'ome?

"Mama?" Eloise sighed but her mother cast her a scathing look which stopped her from uttering another word. They needed the money more than the rest.

"It's only a few more hours, Ellie," her mother hissed. "You'll make do."

The door opened and Eloise found herself wedged between three stinking, drunken lads, not unlike the driver himself, as her mother sat primly on the other bench, ignoring their open leers. None of them bothered to speak and for that Eloise thanked God. She was unsure she would have been able to maintain any level of conversation with them in her current state of mind. Laura stared at her daughter, trying to read her inner thoughts.

Think of the coin and what it can do for us, her mother seemed to be saying, but Eloise could think of little other than how much further the carriage was taking them from their home in the East End and how much longer their day was going to be now simply because of this latest development.

CHAPTER 3

*A*fternoon fell over the grey horizon, blocking out any inkling of sunlight as the carriage stopped to let out one boy after another. The stop and start of the cab jarred at Eloise's nerves as the men stumbled from the interior of the cab, one stopping long enough to rid himself of his intoxicating stomach contents in a nearby ditch before ambling toward his fine home on the hill, even before the driver started back on his way.

Despite Eloise's reservations about the impending work, she could not help but marvel at the neighbourhood in which she now found herself, the beautiful stately houses growing more and more elegant and grander than the last one. It troubled Eloise that those born into such luxury squandered their good fortune on drink and roguish behaviours. If she had ever been so blessed as to live as they did, she would care for her surroundings and those less fortunate than herself.

The colours appeared more vibrant here, the evergreens alive with rich emeralds, the smoky clouds lined with undeniable hints of silver. Sturdy stone walls surrounded lawns or palatial driveways. Even in the dead of winter, there was a brightness, the organic winter décor enlivening the hibernating nature. Even the dusting of snow that had fallen along the landscape remained pristine and pure, untouched. It was as though God Himself had kissed the land here and everything and everybody within it.

Eloise had imagined living in houses such as these, even before she and her mother had been fortunate enough to glimpse inside them with the few extra cleaning jobs they had garnered. She had never before envisioned the splendour encountered inside, with the quaint furnishings and expensive art. Oh, how wonderful it must be to have a kitchen full of food to sate any appetite, so much that the pantries overflowed to the point that the rat catcher was called upon to keep away the vermin from the tantalising aromas which flooded the properties morning, noon, and night.

Several proud chimneys jutted from the rooftops, each house seeming to boast one more than the next until only Eloise and her mother sat alone in the back of the carriage and the vehicle slowed to a stop before a set of wrought-iron gates, bearing a proud family crest. Eloise strained to look at it through the back window, but it was gone before she could fully see it, and along with it, the idea that she had seen it before somewhere.

The carriage paused and a moment later, the face of the young driver poked through the window as the door opened. He grinned at them, his eyelids drooping a little more, Eloise felt as though he might fall over where he stood.

"I'll leave you here," he informed the pair. "There's a boathouse that way where I'd do well to rest up before my father catches sight of me."

He chuckled and winked at Eloise who blushed and looked away. "How long will it take for you to finish the task?"

His question was directed at Laura who arbitrarily offered him a time, but Eloise barely heard what her mother had said. She was certain that her mother had no good idea how long it might take when neither of them had done a job such as this before. It would take as long as it took.

"Jolly good then," he agreed, skipping off toward the west without so much as a backward glance. "I'll be back in a while."

"Oy!" Laura called after him and he glanced over his shoulder. "The well?"

"Oh." He sniggered again and indicated haphazardly. "You'll stumble directly upon it. If you walk that way…" He pivoted and pointed. "Don't venture any further or you'll walk into my family's estate. I would rather you didn't, being we are supposed to be acting discreetly."

He left them to stare at the devastated carriage, caked in mud and ruined from a boys' afternoon of too much drink and little consideration. The light that remained was rapidly dissolving, a fact that did not escape Laura's attention.

"Come along, Ellie," her mother told her quickly. "We'll not 'ave much time te do this."

She stared at her mother in exasperation.

"Ma, why did ye agree?" Eloise moaned. "We'll never get it finished, not before nightfall!"

"We will if we work fast," she insisted, tossing a soiled rag at her. "Stop yer complainin' and get to it."

Their supplies were depleted from the cleaning they had done already so there were no clean cloths to use. "Go te the well over there and fetch a pail of water. Hurry now, girl. The longer ye dawdle, the longer it'll take."

Reluctantly, Eloise swallowed her protests and moved to obey her orders, knowing there was little she could do but adhere to her mother's demands and hope that the job would not take as long as it appeared.

The young man had indeed wrecked his father's carriage, no part of it was unscathed. The horses were restless and annoyed, their manes coated in dirt, their snorts expressed in plumes of mist against the frigid temperatures as Eloise attempted to smooth their hair.

Her fingers numbed as she worked, with each bucket of water containing ice chips by the time it was dumped and refilled afresh. Twilight turned blue and she shivered uncontrollably, regardless of how hard she scrubbed to keep her blood flowing. It was getting to be too much for her, and she could not stop her teeth from chattering, but she did not complain, as it would do no good.

"We're almost finished," her mother reassured her, catching sight of her daughter's trembling blue lips, concern etched in her dark eyes. "I'd wager one or two more buckets ought te do it. Yer all right, luv. Come on now, Ellie. Let's get through this, all right?"

"Y-yes M-ma," Eloise mumbled, wiping harder at the spokes of the wheels. Her mother disappeared toward the well to replenish the water. Inhaling, Eloise drew back to rub her hands together, rubbing furiously, but it did not help matters.

Oh please, God, she prayed silently. *Please let us almost be finished. I just want te go 'ome.*

The sound of footfalls on deadened leaves spun her around and she gasped lightly, startled to see a figure ambling toward her in the near darkness.

"How are you making out?" the young driver asked. His voice was clearer now, more sober as his face appeared. The nap he had taken had done him good and he was more coherent than he had been earlier. Exhaling, Eloise nodded toward the carriage, suddenly tongue-tied. She could not be sure if it were the darkness or his sobriety that made him that much more attractive, but he did seem considerably more handsome than before.

"My goodness, you've been hard at work," he offered, sounding slightly guilty as his dark eyes raked over the carriage. "I daresay my father won't suspect a thing! I owe you both a debt of gratitude...and of money, of course."

Unsure of how to respond, Eloise merely hung her head, afraid she might say something foolish.

"Where is your mother? That is your mother you're with, isn't it?"

Eloise nodded.

"S-she's off te get more water," Eloise mumbled. "She'll be back in a moment."

The young man nodded and dug into the pocket of his vest, withdrawing a handful of coins.

"Then I shall trust you with these. I must return to the house before someone suspects anything and comes looking for me. I wouldn't want my father to catch you out here before you've finished, would I? That would defeat the entire purpose of this covert operation."

He chuckled, depositing the money into Eloise's frozen palm. Slowly, his warm hand curled around hers, a wide, charming smile forming over his lips, and she was struck by an odd sense of familiarity.

"Your hands are quite cold. You really should work with mittens, my dear."

Eloise flushed and shuffled her feet.

"It's 'ard te work with mittens," she mumbled.

"I suppose that's true," he agreed, holding her hand for a moment longer. She relished the warmth of his skin against her icy flesh.

"I daresay…you'll grow up to be quite lovely one day, won't you?" he mused, the aftermath of the whiskey still wafting from his breath. But Eloise barely noticed the offensive alcohol now, her mossy eyes widening as she studied his face. Her stomach twisted as another memory resurfaced.

Boldly, she stared at him.

"What is yer name?"

He chuckled, bemused by her forwardness, and dropped her hand.

"John Edward Winslow the Third," he replied with the arrogance of all wealthy young men. He leaned in confidentially, grinning impishly. "But my friends call me Jack. You may call me Jack, too, if you like."

Eloise's heart lurched as he spun around with the same silly skip he had used when he had first picked them up on the street and she watched him sashay toward the driveway, leading toward the house. She could not help but watch him, even as the last of the light disappeared. Abruptly, he stopped, peering toward a flowerbed where he leaned down and snatched something from the ground. In the dark, it was difficult for her to see what he was doing but Jack turned back around, striding toward her, his hand extended.

Without a word, he placed the small winter flower in her tangled, filthy dark hair before laughing and hurrying away. Eloise gaped after him in disbelief, her fingers reaching up to touch the pretty mauve flower in her unruly mane. Suddenly, she understood why he had seemed so oddly familiar to her.

"Jack, fetch your brother, will you? We haven't time for this today."

The man's voice rang through Eloise's mind, fleeting and fast as her mother marched towards her.

"What in God's name are ye doin'?" she cried. "There's nary an inklin' of sun left fer us te see. Finish up so we can be on our way, Ellie! Aren't ye the one whose itchin' te be 'ome?"

Hastily, Eloise grabbed the flower from her hair and hid it. She had no doubt what her mother would have to say about such a gesture. She retreated to her task in the carriage, but her gaze darted toward the gate which remained open just behind them, the family crest staring back at her as it had from the moment they had arrived. It had haunted her and now she understood why.

I knew I'd seen it before! she thought, her heart racing wildly as she marvelled with joy at the coincidence. *This is the same family I saw at the shop that Christmas Eve when I received my wooden pony. Jack is the oldest boy!*

It was too strange to be true and yet the flower seemed to confirm it. Just as Tommy had bequeathed her the horse, his much more charming older brother had given her a present of his own. This family always appeared to be there for her on Christmas Eve.

CHAPTER 4

*Q*uickening her movements now, distinctly aware of how fast darkness flooded around them, Eloise's pulse began to race. Silently, she willed Jack Winslow to return so that she might ask him about his brother, the one who had given her the figurine, but she knew he would not be back. There was no reason for him to return, now that he had paid them, and the carriage was in a functional condition.

"Mama, how will we get 'ome?" she asked worriedly, wiping faster at the wheels as her head darted toward the roadway. Without a lamp to guide them on the unfamiliar roads, set back from the city streets, it would be difficult to navigate the path back.

"Less chitchat and more work, child," her mother cried but Eloise detected the hint of nervousness in her tone. "We ain't apt te get paid if we don't do a job well."

Eloise started to tell her mother that Jack Winslow had already come to give her the money but before she could utter a word, Laura shooed her daughter away from the carriage towards the horses.

"It's best that ye brush 'em down," she told the child. "They'll get nervous the darker it gets, and they don't know us none. I'll finish up here and then we'll be on our way. I've already dirtied this next bucket. I need more water. It's the last one, ye'll see."

"Mama—"

"Brush quickly, girl. Stop wastin' time! Do ye want te be 'ere all night?"

Hastily, Eloise stepped away from the cab as Laura snatched up the pail at her feet for the last time and marched back towards the well, leaving the girl to tend to the horses. With a shaking breath, she rushed in the direction of the horses, but her sudden movements scared the lead horse and the beast snorted warily. Eloise froze, the plumes of smoke like dragon's fire in her vivid imagination, limpid eyes gleaming against the darkness. The animal grunted uncomfortably as she moved in with a broken, brittle brush.

"'Old still," she instructed the animal with as much firmness as she could muster but her well-honed instincts warned her that the animal was displeased. "Stop it!"

Snorting again, the horse bucked up, attempting to free itself of the ties, alerting its companions to the trouble. All three animals grew restless now, bucking and rearing, rocking the carriage as they moved. Alarm spiked through Eloise who had little experience in handling animals of any kind, apart from the endless vermin who made their way into their rented room, searching for morsels of food that she and her mother shared.

"Stop it!" she cried, her voice raising. "I'm only tryin' te brush ye, ye stupid thing!"

She wished someone had given her better instructions on the basics of horse maintenance but how difficult could it be? It was just a dumb animal, after all.

The loudness of her tone only fuelled the horses' anxiety, the whinnying growing louder as she attempted to stop them. Eloise stepped forward, both hands extended to steady the animals and as she did, the lead horse jumped forward, its hooves raised toward her small, defenceless body. Shock coloured Eloise's face as she recognised the danger in which she now found herself. She would be crushed beneath the weight of the enormous creature.

Through her peripheral vision, an apparition scrambled down from a nearby tree and Eloise was certain that an angel had come to take her to heaven above. She had lived out her usefulness in this life and it was time for the next.

Or perhaps it was a demon, come to claim her unworthy soul to the underworld below. Surely a poor filthy urchin was not welcome openly in the arms of our Lord in Heaven. God would not keep company with such riffraff, would He?

Whatever it was, Eloise barely had time to fully register what was happening, even when his shout filled her ears and caught the horse by surprise.

Time slowed as the animal's hooves crashed down, the horseshoes glinting against the freshly risen moon, bouncing off a pile of snow to blind Eloise's eye. Her slender frame hit the ground, landing in a puddle of slushy freezing water, the pansy flying from the folds of her shawl as the brush whipped off into the darkness and out of her hands. Tremors rocked her chilled, terrified form as she rolled over, staring in dismay at the gangly figure in front of the wayward horse.

"That'll do, Bella," he ordered the beast in an even tone, his hand extended and even. "Calm down, girl. Calm now."

Blinking furiously, Eloise struggled to sit up. In her panic and confusion, she grabbed for the discarded flower, clinging to something familiar for comfort in the midst of the chaos as she attempted to make sense of what was happening. The boy, a year or two older than she, managed to calm the irate horses in a matter of seconds, their huffing and snorting easing under his soft but firm words and hands. Shivers raced down Eloise's spine, the fusion of cold and fear commingling in her heart as she finally got to her feet, shuffling closer—although she maintained a healthy distance from the horses, certain that her nearness would only incense them again.

It's him! she realised, the sight of the boy stunning her more. *Tommy!*

He had grown some since she had last seen him, but she would have recognised those gawky, protruding ears and oddly shaped head anywhere, even if his face reflected none of the awkward charm it had borne the last Christmas Eve she had seen him, outside the toy shop.

"I-I thank ye!" she gushed, stepping forward and then back again, rocking on her heels as she eyed the horse worriedly. She did not wish to provoke the animal again with her closeness, but she also longed to throw her arms around the young boy in gratitude for having saved her. She saw now that his solid push had thrown her from harm's way—even if it had landed her in a puddle of cold grimy water.

He whirled around to stare at her, his dark eyes narrowing in the most unfriendly manner.

"You're a fool!" he snapped, shocking her. "Have you no sense? You cannot yell at the horses! You'll spook them!"

Hurt, Eloise's mouth gaped open, but words did not escape. She did not understand why he was so upset with her.

"W-were ye watchin' me from that tree?" she blurted out, nodding towards the nearby branches where she was certain she had seen him descend. He must have been there for hours, studying them as they worked without her or her mother being aware of his location. Even in the low light, she caught the crimson tinge of his cheeks.

"It's all right if ye were," she added quickly. "Ye saved me—"

"Be quiet!" he called out, cutting her off. Without another word, he whirled around and fled the area, the crunch of his shoes against the dead leaves and snow lingering in her ears as she gawped after him in stunned surprise.

"What in God's name was that about?" Laura panted, hurrying towards her daughter, the pail of water sloshing over the side. Eloise balked to see her mother so close on Tommy's heels and moved to help. "Who was that now?"

"I-I think he's the other lad's brother," Eloise squeaked, reaching for the bucket. Her mother's eyes widened as they fell on Eloise's outstretched palm. With the reflexes of a cat on an unsuspecting bird, the woman snatched the flower from her daughter's hand.

"And I wager he had this fer ye, right? Small wonder he hightailed it out of 'ere when he saw me a comin'."

Eloise balked, having forgotten she was holding the flower. She started to shake her head but before she could utter a denial, Laura threw the crumpled bloom onto the ground and stomped on it furiously.

"How many times must I tell ye, girl? Boys are trouble. They are good fer nothing and want nothing good from ye. You'd be wise te remember what I say afore ye find yerself in a situation ye can't soon escape. Trust yer Ma on that subject."

Sadly, Eloise stared at the broken flower, smeared under her mother's holey boot now. She had hoped to bring it home with her and press it together in her bible for posterity. Once again, she had lost a gift from the Winslows.

"Look at me, Ellie."

Reluctantly, Eloise raised her head to meet her mother's eye.

"Promise me ye'll never again accept gifts from boys— particularly not them with money, right?"

"All right, Mama."

"I want ye te promise me, girl!"

"I promise, Mama."

"I hope ye have better sense than me, Ellie. Now git te work. It's almost to dark te see."

CHAPTER 5

SEVEN YEARS LATER...

I should've known that I wouldn't stay warm for long, Eloise thought miserably, quickening her steps along the cobbled streets, her calloused hands curled firmly around the bucket in her left hand. In her right, she carried a mop and broom, a sack of rags hung from her strong shoulders. Her strong muscular arms brushed against a passerby who immediately apologised.

"Pardon me, sir...uh, ma'am." His eyes brightened with interest to see the comely face of the young woman crossing his path, but Eloise paid him no mind, even when he attempted to catch her attention again.

"My, you're well built for a young lass!" he called. Eloise rolled her eyes, grimacing slightly at the strange compliment. It was hardly the kind of comment she aspired to hear but that was the least of her concerns these days.

She had no time for such flirtations when her mother waited for her to return home.

"Oy! Come back here, flower!" he yelled out, but Eloise had already walked to the other side, her long legs brushing against the coarse material of her grubby dress, the clink-clank of the bucket echoing in her wake.

Even if she had found the man appealing enough to stop and talk, she could not have. After yet another day of working in several businesses, in the West and East End, her labour was far from over. There was still supper to be made, beds to be changed, perhaps laundry to be done, and rags washed for the next workday.

Adjusting the bag on her shoulder once more, she moved in the direction of the boarding house, just beyond the row of dingy grey structures to her right. Once, they had boasted shops of some kind, a toolmaker or a butcher, if Eloise recalled rightly, but it had been years since anyone but the urchin children that roamed the streets had seen the interior of the buildings.

"'Ave ye a coin, Ellie?" one filthy-faced boy cried.

"I gave ye one just yesterday, Jimmy," she scolded him without slowing her stride.

"Yeah, and I spent it on a bun from the bakery," he replied. "I'm still 'ungry."

"Ain't we all," she muttered, shaking her head. Her heart ached for the child as much as any of the others but if she continued to give out money, there would be nothing left for her and her mother, come rent time.

"Please, Ellie!"

"I 'aven't anything te give ye today, Jimmy."

"Bollocks. I hear yer workin' in those fancy 'ouses and businesses in Mayfair now." The child kept pace with her no matter how fast Eloise marched onward, attempting to lose him.

"What of it?"

"Do you mean te tell me that yer fingers don't get sticky now and again?"

Eloise stopped and gawped at him, appalled by his implication.

"What is that supposed te mean?"

"Ye know what it means. They 'ave so much and ye 'ave nothin'. Think of 'ow much ye could 'elp some of us if ye just took a bit o' silver 'ere and there."

"No! Of course not! Stealin' is a sin, James Corneil. Ye ought te be ashamed of yerself for thinkin' like that."

Jimmy was nonplussed by her response.

"Ye mean te tell me ye 'aven't taken a single thing. Not once?" he demanded dubiously. "Or are ye just hoardin' it all fer yerself?"

"I've never once taken a single thing that didn't belong to me," Eloise told him coldly. "And ye shouldn't either, regardless of yer situation. If it ain't yers, ye don't touch it. Otherwise, the law will be onto you."

Jimmy sniffed.

"Yer wastin' a perfectly good opportunity, Eloise Miller. Shame on ye for not takin' advantage when so many of us could use it."

With that he spun around and scampered off to join his gang of street friends as Eloise shook her head in disbelief. She felt no guilt, despite Jimmy's best attempts to make her feel shame. She knew that many in her position had been tempted and resorted to thievery, or outright robbery, on occasion, paying the ultimate price. As long as Eloise was able to work, she would never consider such measures.

I should consider meself lucky that I've never 'ad to resort te it, either, she reasoned. *Ma 'as always taken care of us so that we never 'ad te steal.*

Now, it was Eloise's turn to return the favour to her mother in Laura's time of need.

Sighing, she continued toward the dilapidated boarding house, shoving aside her creeping guilt. The thought of stealing had occurred to her more than once. Would anyone truly notice a missing candlestick or discarded coin if she were to pocket it? It would mean the world to her, pawning a piece of silver that was worth more than most families made in a month or even a year.

But she dared not. For the little good the extra money might do temporarily, in the long term, it could ruin her only means of income, an outcome that Eloise could not afford. Moreover, she was certain that the shame would consume her day and night until she was forced to confess her crimes to whomever would listen. It was simply not in her nature to take what did not belong to her.

Entering the room she shared with her mother, a cloud of black smoke assaulted her lungs as she stepped inside. Immediately, she choked back a mouthful and began to sputter, tears flooding her eyes. Waving her hand in front of her face, she fought her way forward.

"Good grief, Ma!" she cried, hurrying towards the window. "I can barely breathe in 'ere! What're ye doin'?"

Coughing, Laura nodded weakly from her place in the bed, her skinny, pale frame shaking as she struggled to sit up. It was evident that the woman had been lying in the smog for quite a while, unable to do anything about it. The sight of her mother in such a state only enhanced the pity which Eloise felt.

"It took all I 'ad te light the fire," she admitted when she managed to speak a word between her coughs. "The temperature dropped a fair bit over the course of the day."

Sympathy overwhelmed Eloise and she cracked the window a notch to allow for the air to flow and permit the offensive smoke out from the hearth. It did not take long for the harsh December air to consume the smoke from the room and clear the haze enough for Laura's waxen face to become clearer. She appeared worse to Eloise than she had that morning, but the girl reminded herself that it was often the case that her mother looked worse in the evening. The mysterious ailment that had overtaken Laura over the past few months had no name to speak of but it haunted Eloise's every waking thought, and often in her dreams, when she was able to sleep soundly, which was rare.

Eloise turned towards her mother and tried to hide her chiding expression, unsuccessfully.

"Don't look at me like that, Ellie," Laura forced out with far more firmness than Eloise would have expected. "'Aven't ye better things te do than gawp at yer poor old mother?"

Hastily, Eloise shifted her attention away and set her cleaning supplies down, her aching muscles barely noticeable anymore. After so many months of handling all the work on her own, her body had grown accustomed to taking the heavy weight and endless trekking alone.

I'm becomin' manly, she thought sullenly, noting the ripple of her arms as she moved. She thought of the man on the street who had mistaken her for another man before seeing her face.

"What are ye poutin' about?" her ever-astute mother demanded. "'Ave ye given up on me already? Since when do ye take anything I say te heart?"

Surprised by Laura's uncharacteristic display of self-pity, Eloise turned from the small counter, which doubled as their kitchen space, and frowned.

"No, Ma," she reassured her. "I was thinkin' of how unladylike I've become with my potato sack dress and big arms. I'll soon grow a beard and moustache at this rate."

Laura snorted and sank back against the flat pillow, rolling her chocolate-coloured eyes heavenward.

"Thank God for small favours," she replied. "A comely lass asks for nothin' but trouble, I assure ye."

Eloise swallowed a groan of despair, sensing what was about to come. She had heard this lecture far too many times for her liking.

"Yer exasperated with me, but I know what I speak of, girl," her mother insisted. "Bein' pretty ain't what it appears. It's more trouble than it's worth, I promise you that. 'Ard work is a better path for ye. There's no shame in earning yer way. 'Ave we done so badly?"

Eloise wondered how her mother could say that, lying in bed, ailing and unable to afford a doctor. Unable to aid in their finances by claiming work of her own and doubling a meagre income to something passable which barely afforded them rent and food for the most part.

"Wouldn't it be nice to 'ave a 'usband payin' the way now?" Eloise insisted, waving her hands toward the lopsided bed. "Wouldn't ye like to not worry about yerself for once?"

"Ye 'ave no idea what yer goin' on about, Eloise—as per usual. Ye can't depend on the fickle affections of any man, least of all them who 'ave money. Yer best off tending to yer own affairs. There's nothin' that a pretty face will get ye that calloused 'ands won't do better."

Grunting under her breath, Eloise turned back toward the preparation of a simple dinner. It would be leftover scraps and bread it seemed, warmed over the fire.

Yet another happy Christmas Eve, Eloise thought, swallowing her bitterness.

"If ye say so, Ma."

"'Ow de ye think we ended up like this te begin with, ye fool?" Laura demanded, anger colouring her words. Startled by the harshness of her mother's tone, Eloise turned back to look at her.

"What?"

"Yer not a child anymore, Ellie. Surely ye know where bairns come from."

Eloise flushed a peculiar shade of violet, turning her head so that tendrils of greasy, dark hair stuck to her dirty cheek, half-blocking her face from her mother.

"Aye," she muttered. "I know of 'ow babies are made."

"'Ow?" Laura challenged loudly, deepening Eloise's blush. "Tell me."

The girl's mouth formed a small "O" and she blinked, disliking this verbal confrontation, but her mother's steadfast stare did not allow for refusal.

"Well…" she cleared her throat nervously. "When a man and wife are blessed by God—"

"Incorrect!" her mother interjected almost gleefully, a sneer of contempt crossing her face as she again strained to sit up.

"Lay still, Ma." Eloise sighed, moving to set her back but her curiosity was piqued. Had she been informed incorrectly about the mechanics of procreation?

"God and marriage 'ave nothing te do with bringing a child into the world," her mother explained. "Children come te be when they're least expected—and marriage is the least of it. The tales they tell ye are all that—tall tales which prepare ye for nothin'!"

A shiver ran down Eloise's spine. Her mother was speaking blasphemously but something stopped her from stating the obvious. The girl sensed that she was about to learn a secret she had always suspected, directly from her mother's own mouth.

"I was once a fine, young lady," Laura said, a cough punctuating her sentence. Eloise smiled faintly, unsure if her mother was jesting but there was not a hint of amusement on Laura's face.

"In fact, I looked very much like ye, but for the eyes. Me clothes were finer too."

Tentatively, Eloise perched on the edge of the bed, worried that a sudden movement might deter her mother from completing her thoughts, but the woman appeared lost in her own memories. A small frown downturned the edges of her full mouth, a deep sadness etching her eyes.

Is she goin' mad in her illness? Eloise wondered, terrified at the notion. She would not know what to do if that were the case. She could barely keep the pair afloat as it were without her losing her wits.

"I'm sure ye were a very comely lass, Ma," Eloise offered sweetly.

"No, child," she scoffed. "I wasn't merely comely, but well-to-do, as well. Me family had means, and if not for the Morris's, ye would've 'ad a different life."

Eloise inhaled sharply.

"He got me with child without the benefit of marriage, charmin' me with his promises and vows," she went on bitterly. "And I was too young and daft te know any better."

Shame flooded Eloise's soul, but a part of her had already long suspected the truth and she pursed her lips. She was a bastard, a fatherless wretch, unwanted and discarded but for a mother with loose morals.

"Me family was disgraced, and immediately cast me out onto the streets the moment me mother caught wind of me condition," Laura went on, turning her head away. Even after all these years, the pain of her alienation was evident. A sense of deep alarm sprang through the girl's heart.

Why is she tellin' me this now? After all these years? Is she feeling so poorly that she needs to confess the truth?

She could not bring herself to ask the question aloud and instead decided to ask another, one which had weighed on her for a decade.

"The man in the West End, all those years ago," she asked, leaning forward to reach for her mother's hand. "Was 'e me father?"

Laura blinked in confusion.

"What man?" she asked, genuinely perplexed. Eloise sighed again.

Perhaps she's merely losing her wits.

"All those years back, Ma, when we went on Christmas Eve. The day…"

She pursed her lips and stopped herself from saying what she was truly thinking.

The day that Tommy gave me the wooden horse with the brightly painted saddle, the one that you sold for a pittance.

"The day ye argued with the old man in the street."

Aghast, Laura withdrew her hand.

"Ye couldn't have been more than five years old!" she claimed, her eyes widening. "How do ye remember that?"

Eloise shrugged lightly.

"It was cold," she offered, and Laura snorted.

"All our days 'ave been cold, Ellie." Eloise could not argue with her mother's rational, but she noticed that she purposely avoided answering the question which furthered her belief that she had harboured for all these years.

Could I 'ave been so close te me own father and not have known it?

She reckoned that at age five, she had no sense for such things, but now, at the age of fifteen years, a deep sense of loss overwhelmed Eloise, her tired shoulders sagging as she stared imploringly at her mother, begging silently for answers.

"Was 'e?"

Disgusted, Laura threw her head back and scoffed.

"No, of course not," she cried. "That man was much too old te be yer father. What've ye been thinkin' of me all these years?"

Disappointment enveloped Eloise, the loss turning to despair once more. The emotional toll of her mother's tale was wearing on her already frayed nerves, and she rose from the bedside to continue preparing supper, shaking her head.

She is takin' leave of her wits. It's the only explanation.

"That was his father."

Eloise spun back around, her eyes widening.

"Say that again?"

"That was yer father's father—yer grandfather, I suppose." She snorted at the endearment and sunk into the bed, her skinny frame almost disappearing amongst the threadbare bedding. Eloise's pulse raced, her mouth gaping.

"Don't ye go getting excited," her mother warned, reading the expression clearly on her daughter's face. "He made yer father's intentions clear. No one in that family has any interest in getting involved with ye or me, rest assured. He merely confirmed what I already knew."

Eloise swallowed thickly. She had already suspected as much and attempted not to let her disappointment show.

She returned to her mother's side, grabbing for her mother's trembling hand.

"We 'ave one another," she reminded her. "That's been good enough for fifteen years and it'll be good enough for the rest of our days, right?"

Her mother smiled but it came across as more of a grimace.

"Anyway, Christmas is upon us yet again," Eloise added brightly.

"And what of it?" her mother cried. "Without money for a proper feast or gifts, or even a wreath for the door, what makes it any different than any other miserable bloody day in the wintertime?"

Eloise was loathed to admit that her mother was right, but she refused to feel down.

"We'll make do, as always, Ma," she murmured, squeezing her shaking hand. "Ye need te focus on yer recovery though, right?"

"Ye think I 'aven't been tryin'?"

"Ye need te eat," Eloise offered primly, rising abruptly before her mother could see the tears forming in her eyes. Every year, it grew harder to pretend that all would be well. Life would never become easier for them—of that, Eloise was certain. It was getting harder and harder to discover the magic that had once embodied the atmosphere at this time of year, regardless of their impoverished environment.

I'm too old for fairy tales, Eloise realised. *Ma is right. It is better to face the reality of the world around us.*

And yet Eloise knew that she could not let go of it, not this year. There was one tradition that she could not release. Perhaps this would be the last time though.

CHAPTER 6

*E*loise longed to ask her mother more about her father and grandfather, the mysterious Morris family who had never been named until that evening, but she saw how much the short conversation had already drained her mother and decided to wait on her questions.

She remained steadfast in her convictions that, if she was disclosing these deep family secrets, her health was much poorer than Eloise had initially imagined, and the notion gave her pause for the future. Until that night, they had merely existed from one day to the next, doing what was required to survive. Yet they had always had one another on whom to rely. Never had Eloise envisioned a life where her mother was not part of it, not even those months where she had been confined to bed, unable to stand for long periods of time.

Whether it was naivety or the unyielding bond of mother and child, a future without her Ma seemed insurmountable.

But it was commonplace in the East End. Half the children Eloise knew were orphans, running together in bands, formulating new families of their own to replace the ones they had lost.

Will I become one of them? she wondered, tucking one of the frayed blankets around her mother's slumbering frame. A small spool of dribble dripped from the corner of her mouth and Eloise took care to wipe it away with a dirty handkerchief. The sheets were in dire need of washing but there was no time, nor soap, for such luxury. The smell of sick commingled with the thick smoke still lingered in the room.

Small snores emanated from her mother and Eloise sank back onto her haunches, peering intently at her lifelong companion with compassion and concern.

Without a doctor or proper medicine, clean sheets, or a sterile environment, her fate was likely sealed. Perhaps she would not die today from whatever ailment plagued her, but her health would deteriorate and, eventually, the vermin and germs from the streets would overtake her overworked, exhausted body.

Sighing heavily, Laura rose, attempting to shake off the morbid thought this Christmas Eve. This was not the night for such ideas—if any night were. Smoothing the front of her ratty outfit, she again looked towards her sleeping mother. Satisfied that she would not wake again for a long while, Eloise backed out of the single room with as much quiet as she could manage, grabbing for her tattered shawl to drape around her shoulders.

It was only a couple of years old, this shawl—created by her mother's own hand after months of gathering wool scraps from houses that they had cleaned to produce a new, warmer garment for her daughter after her last shawl had been reduced to threadbare rags.

This piece was already worn, despite her mother's craftsmanship, but that did not diminish her work. The item had coped with all of London's unforgiving elements, clinging to Eloise's sinewy frame in every season.

Will I ever own a coat?

The journey had begun already, her worn boots tapping unevenly along the abandoned streets, a full moon heightening in the sky above. The silly, childish traditional habit she continued played in her mind as she walked, her arms wrapped around her upper body in a vain attempt to keep the chill from reaching her skin.

Will I be a fine lady one day, living in a 'ouse in Mayfair with servants of me own? It was a game she often let filter through her mind.

The fanciful questions were rhetorical, meant for fun and giggles, but tonight, Eloise did not feel much like laughing. It was not merely the bitter cold seeping along the crevices of her shawl and onto her bare skin, showering her in goosebumps to cover her from stem to stern. That deep chill never seemed to go, not even in the peak heat of summer, as if her soul had grown too weary to feel warmth any longer. At fifteen, Eloise had known too many hardships to truly believe in miracles any longer. She was not a child, inspired by the wonder of snow and intrigued by the holy story of Christ's birth. The state in which she had left her mother, the discussion about her father, all left a bitter taste in her throat.

It's Christmas Eve, she tried to remind herself, but the tired argument did not carry the same weight that it had all the other years she had trodden across the shadowy, frozen streets, in the middle of the night to enact the tradition that only she knew about.

Perhaps it was time to put it to rest. Faltering a moment, Eloise looked up to garner her bearings but realised she had already trekked much further through the abandoned streets than she had noticed. The West End loomed brighter before her and, despite the endless day behind her, her muscles aching and exhausted, she plodded onward across the cobblestones towards the now-familiar street where Pringles toy shop resided.

It surprised her that it remained, even after all these years, but she reasoned that businesses tended to last in wealthier neighbourhoods. There, people had money to purchase wares sold within the walls of the well-kept buildings, unlike the East End which was constantly a barrage of shops opening and closing as tenants were endlessly evicted. Folks here were able to maintain their rents without issue, regardless of the highly priced frivolous items they offered, such as toys and the like, that Eloise had once eyed with so much envy in her youth.

Once or twice over the years, she had ventured inside during opening hours, if only to peer more closely at the finely crafted items she had seen from the street. Her wide-eyed stares had quickly been quashed by vigilant shop-owners who knew the ill-dressed girl had no place in such an establishment.

They were right, of course. Eloise never had the means to purchase even the smallest ornament on display at the shop and later found herself merely standing outside, watching people come and go, remembering the simple act of kindness that unfailingly drew her back to the same spot. Perhaps, she hoped to see him again, even if he had grown to become sullen and angry as he aged. The memory of his shouting when the horse spooked on the family property was still heavy in Eloise's mind, but she could not forsake the notion that he had also saved her from being trampled that day.

Whatever had become of the Winslows? she wondered, draping the shawl more tightly around her shoulders. At this hour, the temperatures had dropped substantially, and she wished she had thought to put on another pair of stockings. The ones she wore had far too many holes and the frigid air seeped into her skin, reminding her how far she was from home. But she did not start back, not yet. The shop was just ahead and not for the first time, she wished she could read the name of the signage. Many times, she had been tempted to ask a well-to-do passer-by of its title, but shame had stopped her from announcing her illiteracy, even though it was as plain as the patches on her dress. There was no need to call attention to her displacement on the street.

It was part of the reason she had started coming later in the evening, when people no longer wandered to and from the interior, the doors firmly closed for the night, the vendors, and proprietors of the neighbouring shops undoubtedly tucked in their beds, awaiting Father Christmas' arrival.

Eloise turned her mossy eyes skyward, noting the clarity of the sky. The moon glowed with a peculiar halo, but it did not prepare her for the unexpected shadow which fell upon her, reeling her into the gutter.

Gasping, she held up her hands in alarm, recognising the danger she had put herself in by wandering around alone at that hour. A dozen terrible thoughts crossed her mind at once, but they all dissipated the moment he spoke, revealing his face through the shadowy darkness.

"Forgive me," the man called, stepping into the flickering light of a nearby streetlamp. His dark eyes shone with sincerity, and he drew no closer. "I did not mean to startle you."

Exhaling, Eloise took in his fine suit and well-groomed dark chestnut hair, a glimmer of familiarity striking her.

'Ave, I cleaned 'is 'ouse?

It was the logical answer. There was no other reason for her to recognise such a finely dressed and dashing young man. Yet a tug at her heart spoke to something deeper, subliminal, which she could not easily place.

"You needn't be afraid," he added when she did not respond. Eloise managed a curt nod.

"I didn't expect no one out 'ere at this time of night," she admitted. "No 'arm done."

"I could say the same about you!" He chuckled. "Are you all right?"

Eloise nodded quickly, reclaiming her composure as she cocked her head to the side, the sensation that she knew this young man overwhelming her more. "'Ave we met?"

She blurted out the question before she could consider her words, blushing at her own boldness. One did not simply question a member of the upper class in such a way, but he was nonchalant in his response.

"You were at my family's estate, some years past," he replied as Eloise's eyes widened in surprise. Her initial thought had been correct. "To clean a terribly mistreated carriage—"

Understanding flooded Eloise's soul and she began to giggle.

"—which ye and yer friends made quite a mess of, if I recall." She laughed softly. "Did yer father ever discover the truth?"

He maintained his polite smile, and his distance, as he stared at her, causing Eloise's flush to deepen under his scrutiny. Jack Winslow had grown much more handsome than she remembered but a girl's perception at age eight to that of age fifteen was not the same. He neither answered nor ignored her query as he drew nearer, but Eloise held her stance, no longer flustered by his presence, despite the odd hour of the night.

"What brings a young lady to this district at such a late hour? Surely you haven't been looking to shop for something last minute, knowing that it's Christmas Eve."

Eloise lowered her gaze and shook her head, embarrassment clouding her vision.

"I could ask ye the same," she challenged him. "It's 'ardly a proper time for a gentleman te be out and about."

She did not smell drink upon him, nor did she detect any hint of inebriation, either, as she had the last time she had come into his company, but she could not imagine any other reason for him being in these parts at this time of night.

"I've been awaiting a lady," he explained. "And I've been here most of the day, anticipating her company."

She raised her head in disbelief.

"Truly?" she demanded, refusing to accept that a man of his standing would simply stand about in a street all day, waiting on any woman, regardless of who she might be. "Is she the Queen?" she asked jovially.

Jack began to guffaw, but he quickly stopped himself, shaking his head when he read the perplexed but wary expression on her face.

"No," he reassured her. "I suspect that the Queen would have sent word if she was going to be this late."

"I don't know why ye've bothered to stay so long," Eloise told him sternly.

This is one lucky 'en and she's squandered 'er chance with 'im. Pity that.

"Ye ought te go 'ome if she 'asn't come. There's not a soul in sight. She's not apt te come now."

"Oh, but she has already arrived," Jack replied quickly, confusing Eloise further. "She's finally here."

The girl stepped back as Jack fully smiled now, displaying a wide, white row of teeth that blinded her against the darkness.

"W-what are ye talkin' about?" she mumbled, although she began to understand what he was saying, even if she did not comprehend how exactly.

"I must say, your manners are usually much better," he went on as Eloise gaped at him. "You would show up earlier in the day in years past. Albeit, you have come later and later as you've grown up. I feared that one day you would simply cease to come."

Inhaling a shaking breath, Eloise merely gaped at him, unable to find her voice.

"However, I am overjoyed to find myself speaking to you at last," Jack concluded. "I was beginning to think I had conjured you up in my own head."

He peered closer at her, his breath warming her frozen cheeks.

"You are real, aren't you?"

"Y-yes," Eloise mumbled, finally finding a word to speak.

"Good. But that doesn't mean that you still cannot be what I believe you truly are."

Dubiously, Eloise continued to stare at him.

"What do you believe I am?" she whispered, unsure of her herself in that moment.

"Well, Miss, I daresay that you must be a Christmas angel, of course, for that is the only time you appear to manifest."

CHAPTER 7

*E*loise gasped a second time, this one filled with shock and awe. Surely Jack Winslow could not have waited for her all this time, not only today but all the years past, as well. Yet as she stared intently at his earnest face, she read nothing but the truth as he bobbed his attractive head, willing her to believe him.

"I assure ye, I'm no angel," she muttered, feeling heat flood her body. She was certain she had never been so warm on a winter's day than she was in that moment, relishing the mortification of Jack's intense, watchful gaze.

Could 'e truly 'ave been watching me all these years? Why would he do that?

She boldly asked the question aloud, afraid of the response. Yet her curiosity overrode her concern.

"Why would ye wait on me?" she demanded, unable to keep the accusation from her words. "I'm not so very interesting."

He appeared surprised by her proclamation.

"I beg to differ," Jack replied. "In fact, I find you very charming indeed. True, your clothes leave a lot to be desired, but beneath them I can see a person with true spirit and empathy."

Eloise choked on her amazement. Never had anyone referred to her in such a way and if the words were not coming from this man's mouth, she would be apt to spin on her heel and head into the darkness, disappearing from his view forever. But she could not deny that there was a certain mystery to having encountered the young man for yet another year.

"I'm 'ardly interestin' in any respect," she insisted, folding her arms tightly over her chest and stepping back.

"That's simply untrue," Jack countered. "You have many interesting attributes."

"Such as?" Eloise found herself intrigued now, unsure, but committed to this odd conversation, despite the chilling cold, in the middle of the otherwise quiet street.

"Perhaps it is the way you fuss with the fringes of your shawl when your nerves are fraught," Jack offered, nodding toward her fingers. Eloise immediately stopped working her hands, blinking as she recognised his words as the truth. "Or the fact that I rather like your lovely hair, even when it is windblown and unkempt."

Her fingers instantly moved to smooth the tangled braid that had fallen loose in the wind. She had not bothered to comb it before leaving and humiliation burnt through her body.

"But most of all, I like your smile," he concluded.

"What of me smile?" Eloise asked defensively, suddenly very self-conscious of her appearance. Jack's own grin grew, and he shrugged nonchalantly.

"I find your slightly imperfect teeth most charming, the way the crooked one tilts only slightly over your otherwise perfect row. And the way you chatter to yourself when you believe no one else is within earshot gives me great pleasure. It gives me more opportunity to peek at that very tooth, I suppose."

Eloise's jaw dropped, cold and warmth washing through her as she recognised that he had indeed paid very close attention to her habits in the past. Self-conscious and vaguely alarmed, she again stepped back but she realised she was not afraid in the least. For all his observations about her, she did not feel vulnerable.

His attention was flattering but daunting, unbidden, and foreign. She did not know what to make of it and her mother's never-ending warnings of men—particularly those with means—echoed dully in the back of her mind. Yet Eloise could not bring herself to move away. She liked being in Jack's company, even if she understood it was wrong and strange on many levels. Nothing could come of this— certainly, nothing good. If she had any sense at all, Eloise should move along and never return to this street.

Haltingly, she merely eyed him, unsure of what to say or do next.

"I daresay, that you think me rebellious, Miss Eloise," he went on. Her head jerked back again, blood rushing through her.

"Ye know me name?"

"I heard your mother call out to you the day you cleaned the carriage," he admitted. "Ellie, I think, is it?"

Clearing her throat, she lowered her gaze again.

"If ye've seen me so often, why did ye wait te talk te me again for so long?" she challenged. "Ye saw me comin' 'ere every year?"

He nodded and now it was Jack Winslow who looked away, a glimmer of shame touching his expression.

"Perhaps, I feared I would be ill-received," he admitted. "It did take some courage to address you."

Her shoulders stiffened, her eyes narrowing in disbelief. She could hardly believe his excuse. The drunken young lad who had stopped his carriage in a ditch had shown little shame the last time they had met face-to-face.

Perhaps it was the drink which made 'im brave, she reasoned but the answer did not sit well with her. Spirits did not fully change a man, only enhance who they already were.

"I don't see why ye'd need courage te address the likes of me," she mumbled, studying his face closely. He was an upper class gentleman, after all, and she was merely a lowly chambermaid from the East End. Jack appeared stunned by her confession.

"To call on you, of course," he blurted out.

"Call on me?" she echoed, certain he could not mean what he had said.

"Indeed. I've thought of little else since the first time I met you, Miss Eloise. I would very much like to call on you. As often as you'll permit."

"Oh!" It was not the answer Eloise had anticipated and before she could think, her response flew from her mouth. "Absolutely not!" After what her mother had told her about men such as Jack, she had no intention of interacting with him.

Her mother's warning face stood before her eyes, her finger wagging, and her mouth sprouting on about all the terrible tales that men could do to young, impressionable women.

I'll not fall victim like Mama did, Eloise thought firmly. Yet it was difficult to envision this ardent-eyed boy as the manipulator her mother had painted Eloise's father to be.

Jack was clearly shocked by her blunt and candid response, his cheeks paling in the darkness. She swallowed, awaiting a cold or angry retort to her words, but to add to her ill-feeling, Jack maintained his smile and nodded.

"I should have remained in the shadows," he quipped lightly, raising his hand to the brim of his hat. "Forgive me for having troubled you, Miss Eloise."

Abashed and embarrassed by her rudeness, Eloise fumbled to think of the words to rectify her answer, but Jack turned away, clearly eager to put as much space between them as possible in his awkwardness.

"Wait!" she called out, not wanting him to leave in such a manner. If she never saw him again, this encounter would haunt her until her grave, of that, she was certain. Tentatively, he turned but kept the distance between them, the glimmer of hope in his eyes breaking her heart a little more.

I mustn't give 'im impressions. I can't allow 'im to call on me. Mama won't stand for it.

She ignored the nagging question of what she wanted for herself.

"Yes?"

Her mind raced furiously for something to say, something that would alleviate the thick tension between them.

"'Ave ye any familiarity with a family called Morris'?"

Disappointment crossed over Jack's comely features, but he nodded slowly.

"There are two Morris families of whom I'm aware," he replied. "Which one do you mean?"

Eloise wracked her brain quickly, trying to recall any detail about the old man whom she had seen with her mother all those years ago on that very street. Her eyes brightened as she remembered his carriage.

"Their family crest is gold and looks as if it is a tree?"

"Ah, yes," Jack said, nodding. "I know them well."

"Ye know where they are then?"

"Where they live, do you mean?" Jack asked. Eloise nodded, her heart beginning to pound erratically. She had not come looking for answers about her father but inadvertently stumbled upon exactly that.

"Well, yes. In fact, my family is to attend a Christmas party there tomorrow evening. Would you like to join, as my companion?"

Eloise felt as though the wind had been sucked from her breast as she nodded, unable to stop herself.

Oh, this is a terrible idea! A logical voice cried out from the recesses of her mind, but she did not recant her agreement as Jack's face lit up like a Christmas tree, fully decorated with bright candles. He hurried back toward her.

"It will be the most festive occasion with a feast, music and dancing," he went on. "You're welcome to bring your mother—"

"No!" Eloise interjected quickly, balking at the suggestion. Her mother must never know what she was planning, or she would never permit it. Jack stared at her warily and Eloise pressed her lips together. "S-she's not well. She doesn't go out much, these days."

"I'm terribly sorry to hear that. Might I do something to help?"

Eloise's heart lurched, the offer filling her with guilt.

'E's a good man, she thought, cocking her head to the side. *I shouldn't go with 'im te this party under false pretences.*

Yet when would she ever get another opportunity to see her father in the flesh or thank Tommy for the toy horse he had bought her all those years ago?

"She just needs 'er rest," Eloise said primly, avoiding his steadfast, caring gaze and gulping back her shame. "Shall we meet 'ere tomorrow, then?"

"I could collect you at your home—"

"No!" Eloise cut him off again. She managed a smile and shook her head. "It's 'ardly a place for a fine carriage, now, is it."

To her chagrin, Jack reached for her hands and squeezed gently.

"It doesn't matter where you come from, Miss Eloise," he told her sincerely. "It's you whom I find most charming. I have admired you from afar on many occasions."

She wriggled her hands from his grasp and clasped her shawl, knotting at the ends furiously as Jack grinned.

"Seven o'clock," he announced, sensing that he would not win this particular argument. "Right here, where we stand."

"Seven o'clock," she repeated. "Until tomorrow evening."

She turned to hurry off into the darkness as he called after her.

"I would prefer to give you a ride back to your lodgings. The hour is quite late."

Once more, Eloise was taken by his kindness and struck by the distinct difference between him and the boisterous, flirtatious boy she had met on the roadside.

'E's grown into a fine young man.

She did not allow her thoughts to run off with her, tempting as the offer of a ride was on a frigid eve. It was a long, exhausting walk back to their room, but she did not dare allow Jack to know where she lived, nor could she permit the chance that her mother might see him.

"I can manage."

"Of that, I have no doubt!" He chuckled. "Merry Christmas, Miss Eloise."

She paused on the far end of the street and looked back at him, nodding slowly, her pulse still racing from the encounter.

"Ye can wish me that tomorrow," she told him, disappearing off into the night.

CHAPTER 8

It was only a few hours till dawn when Eloise returned home to the shared room where her mother remained in deep slumber, no wiser to her departure than she had been any other year of her toy shop tradition.

The girl exhaled a small breath of relief and hurriedly changed into her warmest woollen clothes before climbing into the bed at her mother's side, but her aching body did not allow for rest. Over and over, she replayed the conversation with Jack Winslow, in her mind, remembering every detail of his words.

Just like Jack, she could not be certain that she had not imagined the entire affair. Perhaps he had never approached her at all, and she had merely been captivated by the hope of Christmas magic, the aspiration for something miraculous to occur on the eve of Christ's birth for once, particularly when she had been so disheartened on her journey to the shop. But the image of him so close was impossible for her to have conjured up in the recesses of her wildest imagination. Never had she dreamt of an encounter with Jack Winslow, even in those weeks following the cleaning of the carriage. Why would a girl of her stature think of something so inconceivable as a boy such as Jack Winslow having the slightest interest in her?

Her mother stirred in her sleep forcing Eloise to realise that she had been fidgeting in her unrest. She made herself lie still, difficult as it was to keep her feet from twitching as she thought of Jack's warm, brown eyes studying her as an artist might gaze at his muse.

Never had she suspected that she had been watched from afar and the more she considered his actions, the more it touched her heart, although what a fine gentleman, such as he was, would find of interest in a vagabond such as herself she couldn't understand. Her whole life, she had never thought of herself as being anyone worthy of being watched, but Jack Winslow had seen something in her that other people had overlooked. She was intrigued by the event the following evening, although she realised it would be complicated to escape her mother's astute notice.

Her own slumber was a lost dream and Eloise rose as the murky grey light of dawn struggled to light the horizon. Flakes of snow danced outside the draft of the windows, blowing a cool breeze inside to stir up the ash along the fireplace. Eloise eyed the diminishing wood pile, mentally calculating the rations for the upcoming week. Would there be enough if she lit another log now or should she bide her time.

As if on cue to her thoughts, her mother began to cough in her sleep, and Eloise hurriedly poked the fire, bringing it back to life, dismissing the cost. Her mother's health was deteriorating, and she needed to be kept warm.

"Good 'eavens, Ellie, what are ye doin' up at this hour? There's not any work t'day," Laura grumbled, turning onto her side when Eloise dropped a tin cup accidentally to the floor.

Apologetically, she glanced at her mother and shushed her.

"Back te bed with ye," she urged. "Yer right. There's no need te rise. I simply couldn't sleep."

"No? Did ye expect Father Christmas te pay ye a visit?" her mother asked caustically. Eloise's heart twinged at the tone, but she shook her head.

"I'll fetch breakfast, Ma," she promised. "Rest now. Ye need it."

"Because I'm 'alf dead, ye mean?"

Aghast, Eloise turned to her.

"Don't speak like that?"

"Why not? It's best to prepare ye for the worst."

Sighing, Eloise joined her at the bed as her mother sat up.

"It's Christmas, Ma," she reminded her. "Can't we 'ave one day of pleasantries?"

"And pretend that all's well?" She snorted. "I thought ye 'ad better sense than that, Ellie."

"Why do ye speak like that?" Eloise asked and her mother blinked once, her dark eyes shadowing.

"Like what? This is me voice."

"But ye come from a fine family. Ye weren't raised te speak as ye do," she pressed, suddenly recognising how much of her life had been a lie.

Her mother paled at the question.

"Why do ye think, Ellie?" she snapped, irritated by the senseless query. "A girl on the East End streets, speaking properly, in lace and silk, would not last a day unmolested. I was forced te do what was required te survive—fer yer sake, and mine."

Eloise bit on her lower lip.

"Surely ye 'ad friends—family members who would've 'elped ye if ye'd begged."

Laura snorted loudly.

"I do not beg! I tried it once, remember, and look what it got me?" she retorted haughtily. "I work—the Miller women, we work for what we have and beg to no one."

Her eyes narrowed as she peered at her daughter.

"What do ye know about my family?" she demanded, anger sparking in her eyes. "Ye 'aven't been foolish, nosing about the West End and askin' about me, 'ave ye, Eloise?"

"No! I wouldn't, Ma."

"Good. Some things are best left as they are. Like yer father. If mine wanted anything te do with me, he'd 'ave sought me out long ago."

Pity for her weary mother gripped Eloise's chest but she had nothing to say to alleviate her deep-rooted suffering.

"Yer right," her mother muttered. "I do need me rest."

She turned over in the bed, deliberately showing Eloise her back as she pretended to go back to sleep, and Eloise was grateful for the small silence that fell between them. She was certain that her mother was not asleep, but it did keep her from questioning her when she moved out into the courtyard later that morning to wash her slightly better smock in preparation for that evening.

When she returned, she was careful to keep it hidden but her mother sat up, eyes gleaming suspiciously.

"Where've ye been, girl?"

"I went te do some washin'." She held up a willow basket, linens falling from the sides as Eloise struggled to ensure they couldn't touch the dirty floor.

"On Christmas Day?"

Eloise averted her eyes, setting the laundry onto the lopsided table and busied herself at the counter to hide her nervous hands.

"It's as good a time as any," she insisted. "There's no one else about."

She was certain the guilt shone through in every word she uttered but while her mother continued to peer at her sceptically, she did not press the matter of the washed clothes.

"I'll be out this eve," she informed her mother in a rush of breath before she could lose her nerve.

"Oh?"

"I've been invited to a party. Do ye mind?"

She cast her mother a sidelong look, holding her breath as she waited for an answer.

"It's already nearly the afternoon," she said slowly. "What time will ye go?"

"Soon," Eloise offered evasively.

"With whom?"

"With a friend I met in the neighbouring tenement."

"What friend would that be?"

Sighing, Eloise turned to face her mother, careful not to lie. She did not wish to mislead her, but it was difficult to avoid the truth with her mother firing such pointed questions.

"Would ye rather I stay 'ere with ye?" she asked tiredly. "I can stay if ye don't want te be alone."

Shame coloured Laura's face and she grimaced.

"I don't need no nanny," Laura grumbled, pulling the holey blankets up around her frail shoulders. "Go te yer party and enjoy yerself."

Relieved, Eloise smiled, perhaps too broadly, again arousing her mother's suspicions.

"Ye are acting rather oddly, ain't ye?" Laura asked warily. "Where is this party?"

A loud knock on the door spared Eloise from having to respond, and she rushed to open it, grateful for whomever had the impeccable timing that Christmas afternoon. Mr Bradberry from the room upstairs stood with a plate in his hands, craning his neck to peer inside the flat.

"Happy Christmas, Miss Miller," he said, offering Eloise a toothless smile. "I've come bearing Christmas shortbread fer ye and yer Ma."

Laura grunted and fully swivelled her body, pretending to be asleep as Eloise stood in the doorway.

"Thank ye, Mr Bradberry," Eloise murmured accepting the pitiful gift. She was well aware of the designs the older man had on her mother. "But me Ma is unwell and not taking visitors at the moment."

The man's face fell.

"Oh. Pity that. Perhaps I could have a gander at her—"

"That is not a good idea, sir. She may very well be catchin'," Eloise told him in a low, confidential rasp. "No one is quite sure what plagues her."

The older man balked at the mention of a virulent infection and backed away.

"Oh. I bid 'er a speedy recovery then," he muttered, again straining to peek at Eloise's lovely mother but she blocked his vision with a cold smile.

"I'll let 'er know," she promised. "Happy Christmas te ye, Mr Bradberry."

She closed the door before he could respond and set the plate on the table, next to the laundry.

"That man is just like all the others," her mother complained, albeit in a much quieter voice, lest Mr Bradberry be listening outside the flimsy doors. "Relentless until 'e gets what 'e wants."

"'E brought shortbread," Eloise offered brightly.

"I wouldn't dare touch them," Laura moaned. "If ye aren't sickly now, ye'll soon be after eatin' any of 'is cookin', I promise ye."

"Wasn't 'e a cook in a galley kitchen once?"

"Indeed. Which is why 'e hasn't the foggiest notion what a true lady's palate should consume," Laura quipped. Eloise giggled and gently pulled her freshly washed smock from the bottom of the laundry basket, sneaking a furtive glance toward her mother. Her mother's eyes were already growing heavy, too many hours of wakefulness taking their toll on her.

"Rest now, Ma," Eloise urged her. "I'll be on me way soon."

"Ye keep yer wits about ye tonight, Ellie," Laura replied then yawned as she closed her eyes.

"Yes, Ma," Eloise agreed. "I will."

She waited until soft snores emanated from her mother's body before slipping into the cleaned frock, attempting to smooth the wrinkled material to the best of her ability, and wrapping herself tightly in the shawl. She brushed her hair until it shone in the low candlelight—it would have to do; she had no maid to curl any ringlets for her. This night, she had the foresight to don two pairs of stockings, the memory of the previous evening's cold still fresh in her mind. She couldn't help but wonder what Jack Winslow saw in her, after all, she was little more than a street urchin, in her poorly laundered dress.

Perhaps I should've 'ad 'im come for me, she mused after almost an hour of walking. Her legs were growing tired and there was still a distance to go but she reminded herself of what waited for her when she did finally see Jack.

It was not just a Christmas party in a warm house with filling food. It was the potential to see her father for the first time in her life.

What will I say te 'im if we come face-te-face?

She remembered her mother's words.

"Keep yer wits about ye, Ellie."

She would need to do precisely that. No one must know her true reasons for being there, that she was the illegitimate daughter of Mr Morris. Her intention was not to ruin the man's reputation but to know from where she had come.

Ma would never understand my need te do this, she thought, pressing her lips together and marching onward with more determination.

"Hello there!"

She froze at the call, whirling around to see a gleaming black carriage. In her lost thoughts she had made her way across the city to the toy shop without realising, and now, Jack Winslow stood at the far side of the street, bearing a warm encouraging smile.

"I was beginning to wonder if you would leave me to wait again," Jack said teasingly. Blinking, Eloise hurried across the cobblestones to greet him.

"Am I terribly late?" she asked apologetically. She had no sense of the hour.

"Not terribly, no," he reassured her, opening the cab door. He nodded inside. "After you, Miss Eloise."

She glanced back at the deserted street and into Jack's caring, dark eyes.

"Go on now," he urged. "You'll find a gift."

She stood back, paling.

"A gift?" she echoed. "I—"

"Go on," he insisted with a laugh. "You mustn't refuse it until you've seen it."

He took her frozen, bare fingers in his gloved hand and helped her inside where a huge, white box sat. Wrapped in a bow of scarlet, Eloise was afraid to touch it, lest she dirty it with her hands.

"W-what is it?" she asked, and Jack snickered softly.

"I do believe it is customary for the recipient of the gift to open it for themselves, Miss Eloise," he replied sweetly. "Although I should warn you, I merely guessed as to your size."

"Me size?" she repeated.

"Open it!" Jack cried, exasperation lacing his words. With trembling hands, Eloise reached for the lid and gently pried it open. The flicker of the street lamps barely illuminated the interior through the open door of the carriage but even so, she could see the lovely emerald green of the lace and silk dress within.

"I do hope it fits," Jack said worriedly. "Although if it does not, there is not much that can be done about it now."

Her hands dropped helplessly to her sides, and she understood that despite having cleaned her dress, it really was not suitable for any event in where Jack Winslow was going. She blushed furiously, but she was not allowed the opportunity to apologise for her appearance.

"I will give you some privacy," Jack informed her, backing out of the carriage. "I'll stand guard, just out here, should you need me, and you may call me when you are ready."

Then he was gone, closing the door in his wake, leaving Eloise to stare at the beautiful gown in shock and awe. She had seen garments like this in the closets of the ladies whose houses she occasionally cleaned but never had she dared to touch the fine material. In her hands, it did not feel real, sliding over the faint callouses of her fingers.

They wear gowns like this every day!

Inhaling a shaky breath, Eloise peeked to ensure that Jack was not watching and found him standing diligently, like a sentry guard, outside the door of the carriage, his back to her. He did not so much as turn his head in her direction as she stripped off her smock, exposing her torn camisole, and slid gently into the new dress.

It was bigger along the bosom than Eloise required but it flowed perfectly to her ankles, billowing over her legs, the sleeves puffing out to display her strong neck and shoulders. A hot flush wiped away the chill of winter when she opened the door to the carriage and Jack spun around to look.

His face brightened, as if there were a thousand shooting stars crossing his handsome face.

"Oh! Heavens, I knew that green was just the colour for you," he murmured, reaching for her hand, pressing the back to his lips. "It rouses the beautiful mossy-green of your eyes in a way I've never quite seen before."

'E speaks like a poet. 'Ow did I not remember that?

"Shall we go?" he asked, and she nodded, swallowing the thick lump of nervousness in her throat.

"I dismissed the driver for the night," he explained. "I've chosen to drive us myself, if you don't mind."

"I don't," Eloise reassured him.

"Good."

He helped her back into the cab and secured the door before taking over the front bench. In seconds, they were off into the night, Eloise peering into the darkness beyond. She felt as if she were a duchess or princess, being whisked away to her first debutante ball. Certainly, this would be a Christmas she would hardly forget, even if she never saw the Winslows again.

In a matter of minutes, the carriage stopped, there were dozens of other similar black carriages parked before a massive mansion house. It was an area that Eloise did not know but she recognised the smell of old money in the air.

The door opened again, and Jack's gloved hand reached inside to lure her out.

"I…" Eloise faltered, until his face appeared.

"You needn't worry, Miss Eloise. You're my companion. You will find no trouble here on my arm." he told her softly. Every word he spoke reassured her, soothing Eloise to her core and she allowed him to guide her to the ground.

"Oy!" someone yelled as they stepped off the carriage. "Does Father know you've taken that carriage tonight?"

Jack turned and grimaced slightly as a man in his twenties approached, an attractive blonde woman on his arm. She turned her nose upward at the sight of Eloise, but the man winked at Jack's counterpart. He bore an uncanny resemblance to Jack but there was a distinct plainness about him which Jack simply did not possess. Eloise knew who he was even before he was formally introduced.

"Edward, haven't you anything better to do than police the comings and goings of father's fleet?"

"Where are your manners, brother?" Edward demanded, reaching for Eloise's hand. "Edward Winslow, Miss…?"

"Miller," Eloise choked.

"Eloise Miller, let me introduce my brother, Edward Winslow and his encumbered bride, Anna."

"Please te meet ye," Eloise mumbled, hearing how rough her words sounded in comparison to their smooth tones. She blushed, waiting for Edward, or Anna, to comment on her speech but before anyone could, Jack skirted her away toward the grand house, tucking her hand into his arm.

I should keep me mouth shut, Eloise thought, pursing her lips as they crossed over the threshold. Two liveried butlers stood, taking coats and hats. Jack led Eloise through the marble hallway and toward the sound of haunting violins being played in the ballroom. They passed numerous guests all dressed in their finest attire with beautiful glittering jewels around their necks, hanging from earlobes or adorning their fingers. Eloise was astonished by the spectacle as Jack steered her past the ballroom entrance to a drawing room to the right.

"Miss Eloise," Jack murmured in her ear. "This is another of my brothers, Daniel."

Immediately, Eloise recalled the two middle boys, fighting and playing the very first time she had ever learnt of the Winslow family. Now they both had names, as well as the oldest and youngest.

"Daniel, I would like you to meet Miss Eloise Miller," Jack said. Eloise allowed the man in front of her to kiss her hand. Peering more closely at him, she frowned.

"Is something wrong?" Daniel asked, returning her expression. "You don't appear pleased to make my acquaintance."

"No, no…it's not that," she said quickly, flushing at his astuteness.

"You are staring at him quite oddly," Jack conceded. "What is it?"

"'Ow old are ye?" she blurted out at Daniel before she could think about any impoliteness. Daniel burst into laughter, Jack joining in as another man joined them. Neither of them was remotely put off by her query, but the question did trouble Eloise more than she was letting on.

This newcomer was also clearly a Winslow, with the dark hair, eyes, and high, refined cheekbones, but he was the least attractive by far. His face was bloated, and his hair was already thinning. Crows' feet had formed at the corners of his eyes and yet he did not seem terribly old to Eloise.

A peculiar sensation twisted in her gut as she began to do a mental count of the brothers before her.

"What have I missed?" he asked, grinning at the trio. He cast a double take at Eloise, as if he recognised her, but maintained his smile. "And who might this be?"

"This is Miss Eloise Miller; may I present my brother?" Jack offered. "John Edward Winslow the Third."

"My friends call me Jack," the plump-faced man interjected, smiling. "A pleasure, Miss Miller."

"I'll fetch Miss Miller a drink if she's so inclined," Daniel said.

"I'm sure she'll be most obliged, won't you, Miss Eloise?"

Eloise nodded dumbly, as Jack and Daniel fluttered off to find her a glass, leaving the couple to stare at each other.

"Y-yer Tommy, the youngest brother!" she gasped when she was sure everyone was out of earshot. "Not Jack!"

"Indeed, I am," he replied. "Thomas Warren Wilson, Miss Eloise Miller. It is a pleasure to meet you properly and truthfully, at last."

CHAPTER 9

*E*loise was again lost for words as she gaped at Thomas, unable to believe that he had once more managed to surprise her. She was a girl of the streets, after all, accustomed to shocks and twists of all kinds. This man had fooled her without her even being a little suspicious in the least.

"'Ad ye any intention of tellin' me the truth?" she sputtered when Thomas eyed her with worry. It was clear he was concerned that she would react badly to finding out his identity.

"Eventually...yes," he admitted. "But there never quite seemed to be an opportune time. Not when you were convinced I was my more accomplished and handsome older brother."

Eloise's eyes darted toward the chubby-faced Jack who had not aged as well as his youth had promised, and she swallowed her words. Thomas had matured wonderfully from the gawky-faced young boy outside the toy shop, his head growing well into his protruding ears, his funny, awkward smile a brilliant, charming beam. She would never have guessed he was the same boy if not for the circumstance of seeing him in front of his siblings.

"I don't understand why ye didn't just tell me," Eloise insisted, shaking her head. "I feel like a fool, now."

"Oh, no!" Thomas choked, grabbing for her hands. She felt the tingle of warmth through his gloves, but the true heat emanated from his steadfast stare in which Eloise found herself lost. "You mustn't feel foolish. It's merely that…"

He trailed off, as if searching for the words, pressing his full lips together and lowering his chin.

"It's just that you looked at me with much more respect when you believed me to be Jack," he admitted, embarrassing Eloise.

"Ye didn't give me a chance to look at ye in any real way," she complained, and he nodded in agreement.

"You're right," he replied. "I didn't, and I apologise for that. Shall we start again?"

Eloise's shoulders relaxed and she bobbed her head.

"Yes," she said. "I'd like that."

He extended his arm for her to take, and she accepted, allowing him to lead her through the lavish party as if she were the most elegant, wealthiest woman in the room, even though there were many bejewelled guests circling around her. Keeping him close, Eloise murmured the words she had clung to for many years.

"Thank ye for helping me with the horse."

Thomas stopped abruptly and stared at her.

"You recall that?" he asked in disbelief. "It was so long ago."

Eloise laughed shortly.

"Ye act as though I'm often showered with help from rich strangers," she replied.

"It wouldn't shock me in the least if you were," he said truthfully, and Eloise blushed again.

'E truly means that.

To cover her embarrassment, she pinched his arm through his sleeve, causing Thomas to jump slightly.

"What was that for?" he asked softly.

"That was for yer rudeness the day I cleaned yer family's carriage," she said. Thomas groaned loudly.

"I was but a boy," he objected. "And unable to display my emotions in a proper fashion. I hadn't intended to be rude, but my worry for you meant I was a little abrupt."

Touched by his honesty, Eloise merely looked at him.

"I should not have been so harsh with you, and I assure you, I spent many a night afterwards wishing I'd handled matters differently. Although, if you will recall, that moment was quite tense, and I was terrified of what might happen if the mare were to trample you."

"Ye were quite quick te respond," she replied coyly, arching a dark eyebrow meaningfully. "As if ye'd been nearby."

A hint of rose touched Thomas' cheeks, but he boldly held her gaze.

"Indeed, I was," he agreed. "I'd been perched in a tree, freezing the tips of my fingers and toes off as you and your mother worked. I wanted to scamper down and offer you a blanket or hot cup of tea to warm your bones."

Now it was Eloise who wore crimson cheeks, matching the gay bows that contrasted the vivid green wreaths about the fireplace mantle.

"Ye do seem to watch me a fair bit," she chided him to hide her embarrassment, but Thomas did not falter.

"Tis what gentlemen do when they find a lady who catches their eye," he insisted. "And you, Miss Eloise, have captured me since before I even understood infatuation."

Her heart fluttered in a way she had never felt, and her tongue knotted oddly in her mouth. Her eyes darting anywhere but his own bright eyes, Eloise took in the luxurious surroundings for the first time. She had not paid much mind to the elegance of the jewel-laden women and their smartly suited companions, their moustaches groomed with pomade and their shiny embroidered vests which must have cost far more than Eloise could ever dream of earning. In each refined hand sat a glass, a goblet, or a tumbler, filled with liquid gold or amber which would inevitably lead them to lower their inhibitions and behave no better than the street thugs at Stella's Tavern in the East End.

Eloise had learnt long ago that it did not matter how much money one had. Alcohol was the devil's breath, luring the most proper of men into the most improper situations.

Yet she was not afraid, not of the overwhelming wealth or the leering men of whom her mother had warned her time and again. For some reason, with Thomas at her side, she had never felt safer and now she wanted to find out about the hosts.

"W-where are the Morris's? Is this their 'ouse?"

Thomas was unable to hide his disappointment, but his tone remained even.

"I never did ask why you have such a fascination with the Morris family," he replied, raising his brow expectantly. Thomas chuckled when she did not respond. "I imagine if you had intended to tell me, you would have done so by now."

Relieved, she offered him a taut smile.

"Come along then," he said, extending his arm. "There's no sense in standing in one spot all night if you wish to find them. The estate is large, and they could be anywhere by this point in the evening."

He led her through the enormous hallway, keeping her close, and Eloise relished the brush of soft cotton lace at the base of her ankles. The sensation was tingling, sending goosebumps rippling up through her body.

"Are you cold?" Thomas asked. Eloise shook her head. For once in her life, she was warm.

"No," she replied. "Not in the least."

"Tommy, there you are!"

A woman's high-pitched voice rang across the room and a spark of jealousy shot through Eloise, stunning her. She whirled around, ashamed to confront a stately but rather familiar woman.

Mrs Winslow, of course.

She had aged much better than her eldest son, hints of white lacing through the blonde of her neat chignon. Her blue eyes raked over Eloise with confusion and curiosity.

"Hello, Mother," Thomas said, turning to Eloise before she could scurry away. His hand tightened around her arm, as if he sensed her need to flee. "May I present Miss Eloise Miller? Ellie, my esteemed mother, Mrs Eliza Winslow."

"Charmed, Miss Miller." Mrs Winslow nodded, offering the trembling girl a small, nervous smile of her own. "Are you of the Westminster Millers?"

"Who could possibly keep track, Mother?" Thomas interjected but his jovial expression faded as a shadow overcame the trio. Eloise raised her head, and she recognised Mr Winslow immediately.

"Papa," Thomas said stiffly.

"Tom. I didn't realise you were here. In fact, I thought you may have missed yet another outing," the patriarch said sternly.

"It's Christmas, Papa. It's the very time to be with family."

"And yet, you've brought a...companion, one that we have not met before," Mr Winslow said, his eyes narrowing as they rested intently on Eloise. He appeared to read every flaw in her, sensing that she did not really belong. She bore no gold or emeralds; her hair was not well kept, even though she had tried to style it appropriately during the ride over—surely a man of Mr Winslow's standing could see right through the charade they presented.

"Father, I would like you to meet Miss Eloise Miller," Thomas said firmly. "Miss Miller, let me introduce my father, Mr John Edward Winslow the Second."

To Eloise's shock, he grimaced and rolled his dark eyes heavenward. It was clear where all four boys had got their dark looks from.

"Dear Lord, no one calls me that," he grunted, offering his son a reproving look. "Jock will do, my dear girl—if you are so inclined to call me anything. Knowing Tom, he'll whisk you away and we'll never again see you."

Eloise raised her eyebrows and Thomas frowned.

"Jock, what a thing to say!" Mrs Winslow chided him gently. "You make it sound as though our boy is a rampant Casanova. Tom has never brought a young lady home before."

"Mother!" Thomas gasped, paling as Eloise swallowed a discreet smile.

"Indeed," Mr Winslow agreed, nodding as a pensive look crossed over his face, his hand reaching to his chin to consider her words.

"Oh dear," Mrs Winslow said and sighed. "We've embarrassed our dear boy."

"Your boy thinks he will take Miss Miller for some air," Thomas sputtered, his face the shade of lilacs in springtime.

Eloise watched Thomas' interaction with his parents, realising that the whole family were kind and considerate toward others. She recalled their first meeting, when the boys were allowed to choose a gift to take to the children's hospital. They had been brought up to be compassionate towards others and this was evident in the way Thomas looked after and treated her.

"Lovely to make your acquaintance, Miss Miller. I do hope we see more of you!" Mrs Winslow called out as Thomas led her away in a rush. Eloise turned to respond but the woman was too far away by now. Thomas pushed open a set of double doors, a blast of cold air rushing in as he led her toward an icy, abandoned veranda. The coolness felt good on Eloise's skin at that moment.

"Please accept my apology for my parents' behaviour," Thomas muttered, a note of irksomeness creeping into his voice. "They seem to have lost sight of the fact that I have grown up."

"Yes, ye 'ave," Eloise agreed. "Much more than I would've expected."

He offered her a lopsided smile, and in the light of the full moon, for half a second, she caught a glimpse of the awkward little boy in front of the toy shop.

It really is 'im! she realised, stunned to see that she had not truly believed it until that very moment. Their eyes locked and Eloise's breath caught in her throat as she noticed how close he was to her.

"You must be frozen," he murmured, wrapping his hands around her bare shoulders. She shook her head.

"I'm not."

"You look lovely in the moonlight, Eloise."

"I was thinkin' the same about ye," she replied huskily, studying the curve of his lower lip. She had never kissed anyone before, never wanted to, but suddenly, she wanted nothing else but to reach forward and touch her lips against his, if only to know what it was like to kiss another.

"There you are!" Daniel and Jack appeared at the threshold, the younger brother holding out a glass of champagne for Eloise to take. "I've been searching for you with this in my hand!"

Reluctantly, Thomas released her as she hurried to put some distance between them and take the champagne from his brother.

"There truly is a feast inside, Miss Miller," Daniel informed her. "Surely you must be hungry. You're a slender thing, aren't you? Tom, you'd do well to plump her up some."

"Mind your tongue." Thomas frowned protectively, marching forward. "She is fine just as she is. Come along, Eloise. You wanted to meet the hosts, did you not? Let us find them and join in the rest of the festivities. It is Christmas after all."

Thomas took her arm once more and guided her back into the party without another look at his brothers, but she could not resist casting them one more glance. They both smiled happily after the pair, elated that their sibling had at last found himself a companion.

CHAPTER 10

Although her anxiety lingered, it diminished the more she was on Thomas' arm, his nearness lessening the nervousness of her being an out-of-place girl at a lavish affair with the wrong hair and accessories but the proper dress. Never was her rough, blistered hand empty of food or drink, her mouth full of delicacies she had never tried before in her life but had eyed from afar.

"What is this?" she asked Thomas on more than one occasion, and every time, he was happy to tell her what she was eating, even if she did not understand half the words he spoke.

"Pate," he explained. "Caviar." A multitude of other exotic sounding foods were presented to her in the same way.

Some of what she tasted popped against her taste buds, causing her eyes to widen in shock. Food had never had such an effect on Eloise before. Its function had never been for her to enjoy, not truly. In her experience, food had only ever been a necessity to end the pitiful growling in her stomach but never to fully know the flavours that danced with joy in her mouth. Could nourishment be more than simple sustainability? If so, Eloise had never understood it until that moment.

"Ah." Thomas sighed. "I could watch you consume watercress sandwiches until the end of my days," he whispered. The heat of his breath on her neck and ear sent shivers down Eloise's spine as another flush crept along her arms.

"Whatever is watercress?" she replied softly, causing him to howl with laughter. The sound attracted the attention of yet another curious group who eyed the couple with a fusion of contempt and curiosity.

"We've made quite a spectacle of ourselves," Thomas joked lightly but Eloise sensed no shame in his tone. "Shall we make one more?"

She stared at him uncomprehendingly.

"W-what do you mean?"

He nodded toward the orchestra who had begun to play a pretty lilting tune and several couples had taken to the floor to begin a waltz.

"Will you dance with me, Eloise?"

Aghast, she began to shake her head.

"I-I don't know 'ow!"

Thomas was unperturbed by her claims and took her hands, setting her drink aside on a nearby table.

"It's really quite simple," he assured her. "Follow my lead."

Perhaps it's simple for 'im! 'E's been doin' it 'is 'ole life.

"It's a mere three steps, really," Thomas explained, pulling her close. The proximity of his body stole her breath, but she did not pull away, her chin jutting back to stare up at him as if she were a deer caught in a hunter's sight.

Thomas offered her a reassuring smile.

"You needn't look afraid, Eloise. It's merely a dance."

'E says that as though I dance every day!

Slowly, Thomas began to shuffle his feet forward, stepping on hers and Eloise gasped aloud.

"When I step forward, you move your foot back," he explained, unable to keep the chuckle from his voice. Defensively, Eloise started to shrug him away, but he held fast to her.

"Try it again," he insisted. "I suspect you'll be rather good at dancing if you would only give it a chance."

She paused and stared at him inquisitively.

"What makes ye say that?"

He shrugged slightly.

"You're quite good as slipping away, and that takes a certain amount of grace, does it not?"

In spite of her defensiveness, Eloise relaxed.

"Come now," he pressed. "Let's try again."

Inhaling, she focused on his movements and allowed him to start once more.

"When I move my foot toward you, you move your foot back. Likewise, when I move my foot back, you move the appropriate foot forward, yes?"

She nodded. Suddenly, she was distinctly aware of several sets of eyes upon her in the room and a fine perspiration formed on her brow.

Most of the attention appeared to come from other prettily dressed young ladies, each of their faces fraught with envy that she was in the arms of eligible bachelor Thomas Winslow, and they were not.

It seemed strange to Eloise, too, that Thomas had blossomed into such an attractive young man whilst Jack had turned out to be sallow and plain. If she had wagered on who would have become the more attractive brother, she would have lost. There was no trace of the oversized ears and gawky grin that Thomas had once borne as he confidently swept her along the dance floor, her own steps gaining surety under his guidance.

Breathlessly, she spun around, the faces before her becoming a blur until all she could see was Thomas' smiling face before her, all else forsaken.

Abruptly, the music ended, and the throng of party guests moved away. Thomas gently released her. Disappointment flooded her soul as he did, but she willed herself to behave properly. She had not wanted to dance in the first place, she reminded herself.

"Oh," Thomas called, raising a finger slightly. "Look."

She followed his stare blankly but even before he spoke, she understood what he was pointing at. The old man who had just entered the room, was much older now, his face as grey as his thinning hair, his body hunched over a wooden cane that possessed an ivory handle carved in the shape of a serpent. It appeared as if it were the only thing keeping him from collapsing to the floor entirely.

"There are the Morris's."

Uneasiness struck Eloise's stomach and she wished she had not been so bold, so careless, in venturing to this party. She was in their home, uninvited, on Christmas Day. What had she been thinking?

And… what if old Mr Morris were to recognise her?

Don't be foolish! she scolded herself. *'E 'asn't even laid eyes on ye before. And if 'e ad seen ye, ye were no more than five years old.*

Still, Eloise could not calm her quickly fraying nerves, her eyes darting towards the people at her grandfather's side. He stood amongst two tall gentlemen and a refined young lady; all a generation younger than he was.

Are they related to 'im? Could one of those men be me father?

Her eyes narrowed speculatively, taking in the gentlemen with closer scrutiny. They both had dark hair, the woman too, but that meant little. Many people had dark hair, as she did. She longed to get closer and peer at their faces, to search for any resemblance between herself and the men.

"You shouldn't stare, Miss Eloise," Thomas chided her gently. "It's impolite."

She had almost forgotten she had an audience of her own.

"Why are you so interested in the Morris family?" Thomas wanted to know. "You never did tell me."

But before Eloise could pull her eyes away, one of the men suddenly jerked his head up as if he felt her gaze upon him, resting his own eyes on her. The mossy green of his stare caused her to gasp aloud but his mouth formed a horrified "O" of surprise. Even from that distance, Eloise watched the blood drain from his face. He lurched forward in his shock, the crystal tumbler in his hand slipping to spray over his companions, as he moved to catch it—but he was too late. The drink fell from his hand, crashing to the floor with a loud smash and, immediately, servants rushed to attend to the broken glass, almost before it touched the ground.

The other man and woman drew back with cries of alarm as the old man reprimanded him in a reproving, fatherly way.

Trembling, Eloise pulled out of Thomas' arms, shaking her head in disbelief, her eyes locked on the shocked expression of the younger man's. His mouth formed a word, one that she could not hear but understood.

Laura.

His expression told her everything that she needed to know.

"Eloise?" Thomas' voice was etched with alarm. "Are you all right?"

She was unable to answer, her feet falling over one another as she backed away, eager to put as much space as she could between herself…and the man she believed to be her father.

CHAPTER 11

⧡

*E*loise did not know where she ran, her boots flopping about her feet as she rushed away from the sounds of the orchestra, and into another room. Air rushed through the opening, her dark hair falling free of its hold, as she was reminded that her footwear did not match the dress she wore. Everything about her stood out. She could see that now. How did she think she could be accepted by the wealthy echelons of society?

She reeled to a stop in the next room, realising she had taken a wrong turn. Wayward, laughing guests drove her back into a vast hall, and she whirled about, seeking an exit of sorts. Eloise could not be certain if they were mocking her or merely enjoying the party, but the sound of their mirth was synonymous with jeering to her now sensitive ears. Although all the people she had encountered had been cordial at the event, surely, they had been leering behind her back. They had likely held their true opinions out of respect for Thomas.

I'm a fool to 'ave come 'ere! she thought, blinking rapidly before tears could fall down her cheeks. She was distinctly aware of all the eyes upon her now as she moved, unaccompanied, through the house, finally finding the exit she sought through the bustling kitchen where the servants were preparing giants platters of food to serve. Here, she felt much more comfortable, but the workers appeared startled to see her.

"May we help you, Miss?" one woman asked, smoothing her white apron nervously as she glanced at her companions. "Guests shouldn't be back 'ere. It's dangerous."

Without a word, Eloise hurried past to allow herself out of the back door and into the frigid night air. Heavy snow had started to fall from the sky since she had last been on the terrace with Thomas. Cold flakes touched her bare skin, but she ignored them, though the awful chill had threatened to overtake her. Any semblance of warmth she had felt at the party had diminished rapidly now and she had only an aching sense of loneliness as she rushed around the side of the house.

I must get 'ome, she thought, finally stopping at the row of carriages in front of the grand estate. They all looked so much the same, sleek, black, with their pull of shining dark horses. She wondered if she might ask Thomas' driver to take her home and return for Thomas at a later time, but she was unsure which carriage was his.

I know 'is family crest, she reasoned, remembering that her own clothes sat in that coach. Surely, the driver could not turn her away with her belongings inside.

"Eloise!"

The sound of her name forced her to turn around, her cheeks paling at the sight of Thomas heading toward her from the front of the house. Her instinct was to flee but she had nowhere to run, without even a shawl to protect her against the freezing cold. She would never make it back to the East End in her current attire, not without freezing to death.

"What are you doing?" Thomas demanded breathlessly when he joined her side. "You look as though you saw a ghost in there!"

Unable to offer him a proper response, Eloise merely shook her head. How could she tell him the truth about who she was and what she had done? As kind as Thomas Winslow claimed to be, as open-minded as he believed he was, his family would not abide a girl such as her attending lavish parties at their wealthy friends' homes. She was nothing more than a bastard child, discarded by a father who had turned his back on her for fifteen years or more. It was clear that he had never expected to see her again, least of all on his own property. If she dared show her face again, what would he do? Although there was one thing for certain, she had no intention of ever finding out.

"Eloise, you must tell me what is going on," Thomas implored her, the confusion growing in his eyes. "You seemed to be having such a lovely time. Did you see someone? Did someone say something to you?"

"I'd like te go 'ome now," she said curtly. "Can ye 'ave yer driver take me 'ome, please?"

Thomas appeared taken aback by her request, his lips parting slightly.

"Come back inside for a short while," he begged. "I'd like to introduce you to some more people."

There was a cajoling note to his voice and Eloise's eyes skirted toward the vast house, her heart lurching at the very sight of it now.

Would this 'ave been the 'ouse I'd 'ave lived in if 'e'd accepted me as 'is daughter? Would me Ma 'ave lived 'ere too if 'e'd married 'er instead of deserting 'er?

A fusion of anger and sadness overwhelmed her. What difference did any of that make now? She was not part of this life and never would be. Playing a pretend game of imagination changed nothing.

"No," she said firmly when Thomas reached for her icy fingers. She pulled back, folding them under her armpits. "I want te go 'ome."

Disappointment coloured Thomas' face and he nodded slowly, his dark hair falling charmingly over his forehead, shadowing his eyes.

"Let me get my coat and hat," he said shortly, not bothering to keep the upset from his words. "And I'll take you."

"Ye don't 'ave te come," Eloise told him quickly, shame flooding through her. "I-I can go on me own."

"Don't be ridiculous." Thomas frowned, turning away. "I'll not let you leave here unaccompanied."

He did not give her a chance to argue, heading back toward the house as she stood helplessly, shivering in the night. A couple exited through the front door, chattering gayly, arm-in-arm. They smiled politely at Eloise as they passed, bidding her goodnight but she could not bring herself to respond. Suddenly everyone appeared to be mocking her and she could not feel a semblance of comfort among the indulgences of the Morris household.

'Ow could I ever 'ave imagined meself 'ere? she thought bitterly. *Ma was right about these people. Why didn't I listen? She knew better than I.*

Yet she found herself looking back toward the party, wondering if her mother's family might be inside. She had not thought to ask about the Millers but after what had happened with the Morris's, she dared not. She had already learned more than she needed to know. She thought of how defensive Laura had been when she believed Eloise had been asking about her kin.

Some things are best left unknown. Why didn't I heed Ma's advice?

She attempted to tell herself that now she had absolution, the closure she needed on the matter. After years of the unknown, she could finally know peace. Then as Thomas reappeared with his hat and coat, her heart sank, and Eloise realised that with this closure came something else. She must never again see Thomas Winslow or maintain her Christmas tradition of going to the toy shop. In one fell swoop, she had managed to ruin any happy childhood memories she had struggled to create.

"I would like you to tell me what is going on," Thomas muttered, offering his arm. She pretended not to see it as she marched forward, forcing him to hurry after her, if he wanted to keep by her side. "I thought the night was going well."

Unexpectedly, tears again filled Eloise's eyes, but she brushed them aside before he could see them.

It's not right that 'e thinks I'm upset with 'im, she thought worriedly, but she could not think of a single thing to say that would alleviate his anxiety. Any words that she could think of would surely make it worse. If she uttered the truth, that Mr Morris' son was her father, it would cause a scandal if Thomas confronted the man. Thomas, being the noble, caring person that he was, did not seem the type to let the matter go without discussion. No, it was best if she said nothing at all.

"I know it must have been daunting, coming here, but Eloise, you were accepted well at the party. Didn't you feel that way, too?" Thomas pressed, unable to take her silence as an answer. The coachman hurried to open the door as they approached, tipping his hat with a small smile but neither acknowledged him as they climbed inside.

"I'm quite tired, Thomas," she mumbled. "Please. I just want te go 'ome."

"Where is home?" Thomas sighed, realising that he would not be able to convince her to return to the party.

"N-Notting Hill," Eloise stuttered, the neighbourhood sticking to the roof of her mouth. Thomas relayed the direction to the driver and the door closed, leaving the pair in relative darkness before the horses began to move. Idly, Eloise wondered if it was the same beast who had almost trampled her all those years ago, but she was in no mood to ask.

It's best to leave the past where it belongs. I'll do just that.

"Eloise, if I've done something to upset you—"

"Ye 'aven't," she interjected. "I'm tired and want te go 'ome, tis all."

She avoided his eyes and peered out of the window, the lamp-lit streets passing by in a blurry haze. There were tears shining in her eyes again.

"Why won't you tell me what happened?" Thomas demanded. "You're acting very strangely?"

She said nothing, knowing that whatever words she spoke would not make matters any better. She was bound only to make things worse if she tried.

"Who are the Morris' to you?" he asked pointedly, and Eloise's shoulders rose, and a shiver rushed down her spine. "Please, will you answer me that?"

She shook her head, refusing to meet his eyes. Thomas exhaled loudly and sat back in his seat, folding his arms defiantly across his chest, accepting that his questions would remain unanswered.

His annoyance was palpable but beneath that, perhaps more predominate, was his concern. For all he had done for Eloise, he was worried about her, and she could sense his worry.

"'Ave the driver stop 'ere," she instructed him abruptly as the carriage started into the Notting Hill neighbourhood. She was not near the boarding house yet but the buildings here were considerably nicer and embarrassment forbade Eloise from having Thomas see precisely how impoverished her life was in comparison to his. Even if she was never to see him again, she still did not wish him to have her decrepit rooming house as his final memory of her.

"Stop here, Henry!" Thomas called out, tapping on the window which separated the cab from the driving bench. The horses snorted lightly as the vehicle came to a standstill in front of a single-family home, the paint peeling pathetically. Thomas moved to help her out of the carriage, but Eloise had already scampered through, relinquishing her own clothes. She was so desperate to get away, to be alone with her thoughts and emotions before she lost control entirely.

"Eloise!" Thomas called after her, but she did not turn around as she sprinted across the street, willing him to leave her be. "Eloise!"

Please, just go! she cried out to him in her mind. *Don't make it any 'arder than it already is.*

The hem of her flowing gown tangled around her ankles as she turned the corner, but she barely noticed that she was still wearing the fine garment. Her only thoughts were of escaping Thomas' compassionate, concerned gaze and being alone.

Goodbye, Thomas Winslow. Thank ye for everything, and please, 'ave a Merry Christmas.

The tears came when she let herself into the room, her mother soundly asleep in the bed, her gentle snores reverberating through the room as Eloise curled up at her side. Sobbing softly, she allowed her tears to finally overflow. They felt lovely on her cold cheeks until they eventually lulled her into a false sense of secure slumber and into a world of haunting dreams where partygoers laughed at her; the poor little girl pretending to be someone she was not.

CHAPTER 12

*I*t appeared as if a bird had flown into the flat during the night, the screeching rousing Eloise from her fitful slumbers. The terrible squawking noise flooded her ears, its beak pecking at her chest and arms. Her eyes flew open to confront the beast, the remnants of sleep falling away as she realised it was not a crow attacking her but her own mother who was clawing ruthlessly at her as if she were a wild animal, her face twisted in a way that Eloise had never seen before.

"What is the meaning of this!" she howled furiously, tearing at Eloise's dress. "Where did ye get this fancy gown from?"

Eloise managed to slip out of her mother's vice-like hold and roll to the side of the bed, silently cursing herself for not having the foresight to change the previous night. In her upset, she had not been thinking clearly enough.

"Tell me, girl!" her mother insisted. "Were you out with a man last night? Is that where you got it?!"

"Calm down, Ma," Eloise choked, her head pounding. Her vision was vaguely cloudy, and her skull felt pressed and uncomfortable, as though she were going to be sick.

And that is all I need...

"I will not!" Laura thundered. "You fool! How many times 'ave I told you te steer clear of men? How many times 'ave I warned ye about the dangers? What did ye do?"

"Nothin'!" Eloise insisted, holding up her arms as her mother leant forward to look at her. "I only went te a party, like I told ye."

"With whom?"

"No one ye know?"

"Oh! Oh, I knew ye were up te no good. I seen it in yer eyes, last night. I should've forbidden it."

Eloise scowled, slipping out of bed to undress.

"Bloody 'ell, what 'ave yer done!" her mother cried. "That dress is worth a small fortune. Be cautious with it. We'll sell it and it'll pay the rent for several months. And I don't want te 'ear any arguments out of ye."

Eloise was in no condition to argue, nor did she care what happened to the dress. She never wanted to see it again. It would only serve as a reminder to her own stupidity.

"You can do whatever ye want with it," Eloise grumbled. "But keep yer voice down, please."

Eloise's eyes narrowed into slits.

"Have ye been drinkin'?" she demanded, aghast. Eloise blushed, remembering the glasses being pressed into her hand throughout the party. She had not realised how much the alcohol had affected her until that moment.

"No," she lied.

"Don't ye fib to me! I can smell it on ye! 'Ow are we expected te find jobs when ye smell like a brewery?"

Eloise scoffed loudly.

"Ye don't find jobs!" she retorted sharply. "I find jobs, Ma. I take care of everythin' around 'ere, remember?"

Laura balked at her daughter's tone, unaccustomed to being spoken to in such a manner.

"Well, that's worse then, innit? Yer the one the mistresses will be speakin' te and no one will 'ire a drunken cleaner t'day, will they?"

"Then maybe I'll take the day off," Eloise moaned, her head swimming. Her stomach lurched slightly for a moment.

"Oh, good grief!" her mother snapped. "Look at ye, all high and mighty with yer rich suitor. Takin' days off now, are ye? And when he knocks ye up and leaves ye with nothin but a bairn? Then what will ye do?"

"I am not ye, Ma!" Eloise yelled indignantly. "I won't make yer mistakes!"

Laura's face turned ashen, and Eloise instantly regretted her words, but she did not apologise. She had not crossed the same lines that her mother had but she should not have thrown her past stupidity in her face as she had.

"Ye don't know what ye'd do until ye do it," her mother replied shortly. "Yer wearing an expensive dress and stayin' out until the wee hours of the night. Yer not in charge of yer wits."

"Ye weren't in charge of yer wits. That's why we live like we do. If ye 'ad been, our lives would've been so much different!"

Laura blinked several times, a mixture of confusion and worry lacing her eyes.

"What do ye mean by that?"

"Ye know what I mean," Eloise grumbled, padding towards the water jug, looking for a cup for water. Her mouth was dry and padded, her throat felt as if it were coated with cotton. The throbbing in her head would not diminish and the quarrel with her mother was not helping matters in the least.

"No, I don't," Laura insisted. "Tell me."

Locating a clean cup, Eloise poured icy cold water from the pitcher and took a long gulp before answering.

"If ye had done what ye were supposed te do, ye would still be livin' in the West End, in a fine 'ouse without 'aving te work so 'ard. Ye would 'ave servants, 'ave a doctor for when you were sick. Now, look at us."

She set the water down on the rickety table with too much force and it cracked the bottom, causing her mother's frown to deepen.

"Ye can thank yer father fer that," she spat back. "He made me promises, just like yer suitor is makin' ye promises right now. I warned ye about this. 'Ow can ye be so bloody stupid?"

Eloise opened her mouth to retort but her words were cut short by the sound of a commotion upstairs. The pounding on flimsy doors caused them to turn their heads upward, the sound of muffled voices filtering down towards them.

Ignoring the noise, Eloise turned back to her mother.

"Ye 'ave a part te play in this too, Ma," she said. "Ye are not a victim."

"Ye think I don't—" Another loud knock stopped her, and again, they looked upward, realising that the person overhead was going from door-to-door.

"It's the 26th of December today, right?" Laura asked suspiciously. Eloise nodded, despite the fact it hurt her head to do so. "Why is Mrs Bellows coming for the rents then?"

Eloise tensed at the question as another knock, this one closer, caused her teeth to clench. They did not have this week's rent and it was too early for the landlady to be collecting.

"Maybe…maybe it's the church bringing alms for Boxing Day," Eloise offered weakly. A loud voice and a slamming door told her that her theory was flawed. Whomever was bothering the neighbours was not welcome.

"Don't answer the door if they come knocking 'ere," Laura urged as they sat in silence. Their fight temporarily forgotten; their ears strained as they listened near to the door.

The unexpected visitor had moved to their floor now and was situated at the room next door. Through the thin walls, Eloise heard Mrs Carol's denial as plain as day.

"Ye 'ave the wrong place, Mister. Next door. The lady lives right next door."

Laura eyed her daughter suspiciously, wild-eyed and angry.

"Your suitor?" she hissed as Eloise paled at her accusation.

"It can't be!" Eloise whispered back. "'E doesn't know where I live, I never told 'im."

"It sounds as though 'e's figured it out!"

Heavy footsteps padded down the hall and under the crack in the door, a faint shadow fell. Eloise inhaled sharply as she moved towards the doorway.

"Don't ye dare!" Laura insisted. Eloise yanked open the door before the person could knock, and she stared directly at Thomas' stunned face. Immediately, she tried to shove the door closed again, even though she had fully suspected that it was Thomas on the other side in the first place. She had only wanted to know for sure and foolishly her curiosity had got the better of her. With startling agility, he leapt forward, jamming his shoulder in the door to prevent her from closing it, shaking his head with a rueful smile on his lips.

"Have you any notion as to how rude it is to dismiss a man who has knocked on nearly a hundred doors this morning in search of the very person they wish to find?" he asked cordially, not a hint of upset in his tone. For a long moment, Eloise could only stare at him, unsure of what to say or do. A million thoughts raced through her mind, the urge to close the door was at the forefront of her mind, then again, maybe she should throw her arms around his neck and beg him for forgiveness for her actions the previous night. She wished dearly to run off and hide in a corner until her throbbing headache finally subsided and she could formulate a proper plan.

Yet none of those notions prevailed.

"What are ye doin' here?" she demanded. "How did ye find me?"

"I just told you," he replied. "I've knocked on every door of every flat in the area in search of you. Truth be told, I was beginning to lose hope of ever locating you."

"Perhaps it would've been better if ye 'ad," Eloise mumbled, dropping her eyes. His lips parted to say something else but before he was able to utter a word, an older man's voice rang out from down the hall.

"Is that her? Have you found her, Thomas?!"

"Who is with ye?" she choked out, craning her neck toward the hall. Eloise reeled back in shock, her eyes popping as the man she presumed to be her father appeared, his mossy green eyes wide and stunned as he took her in. Gasping, she fell against the door, shaking her head.

"Y-ye b-brought 'im?" she stuttered. "W-why would you do that, Thomas?"

From behind her, Laura cried out and Eloise whirled to look at her mother who appeared as traumatised by the events unfolding as she was. Laura's hand reached for her hair as if to primp it, but her fingers fell away to smooth the front of her worn nightdress instead.

"Patrick," Laura whispered as he looked to her and back again to Eloise.

"Oh," Mr Morris sighed, stepping across the threshold uninvited, "you do look so much like your mother."

Once more, his eyes drifted toward Laura who seemed ready to burst into sobs, but she maintained her dignity, straightening her spine and extending her hand protectively toward her daughter.

"But for your eyes, of course," Mr Morris continued. "Your eyes are most certainly mine."

"You have no claim to anything of hers!" Laura shot out indignantly, her words even and proper, stunning Eloise. Never had she heard her mother speak so well, not a hint of the East End brogue she had always known. "Ellie, come to me."

Trembling but obedient, Eloise did as she was told, standing behind her mother as Patrick Morris stood shamed and anguished before them.

"How can you say that, Laura?" he demanded. "She is my child!"

"How dare you?" Laura spat back, the fire in her eyes unlike anything Eloise had ever seen before. She peeked at Thomas who appeared just as awed by her mother's fury as Eloise, the younger generation stepping back to allow the former lovers their time to finally speak the truths long buried between them. "You gave up your right to call her that when you turned your back on us, sixteen years ago!"

Patrick balked at the accusation, shaking his head vehemently.

"That is simply not true!" he declared. "I had no knowledge of Eloise until last night, when I first laid eyes on her at my home. I thought I was seeing an apparition, of you, at the same age when we had fallen in love!"

Eloise snuck another look at Thomas and found him staring right back at her, but he quickly looked away and she did the same.

Could it be so? Could Patrick not 'ave known about me?

"That's impossible," Laura scoffed but Eloise read uncertainty in mother's eyes. "I sent word, and you left the following week without so much as a goodbye."

"Sent word? With whom?"

Laura faltered, her hands working nervously, and Eloise realised that she was also fidgeting with her own fingers as she waited for the rest of the tale to unwind.

"I-I wrote a letter," she explained weakly. "And delivered it to your house. I gave it to the butler."

Patrick groaned loudly.

"Laura, you should have known, Evans is my father's butler and always has been," he moaned softly. "He would not have delivered any such missive to me. He must have delivered it directly to my father."

He paused pensively.

"That would explain the rush to send me away so abruptly."

Laura's knees buckled and Eloise reached for her, but Patrick got to her first, steadying her before she could collapse completely.

"I would never have abandoned you and our child, Laura. You knew how much I cared for you—"

"That's a lie!" Laura interjected, shoving him off. Eloise blinked in surprise. The explanation seemed plausible to her, but her mother was having none of it. "If you cared for me so much, why did you never write to me while you were away?"

"I did!" he insisted. "Every week! It was you who never returned my letters! I thought you were through with me when I left. I had no choice in the matter, but I had hoped you would wait for me. When I returned from Eton, your father told me that you had left for the countryside and married another person who was from a much wealthier family."

Laura grimaced, pain overtaking her eyes.

"That sounds just like something my father would say to save himself the embarrassment," she muttered, shaking her head sadly.

"You must know that if I had any idea that you were living here, so close, and in such conditions, I would have come long ago."

Laura sniffed and righted her body, stiffly walking toward the bed before sitting again.

"You mean to tell me that you never married or had children?"

A long silence followed Laura's question and she chortled mirthlessly.

"Just as I suspected," she offered coldly. "You are a liar, Patrick Morris, just like your father and mine."

"I am not a liar," Patrick forced out from between clenched teeth. "I was married to a woman of my father's choosing. Her name was Miss Mary Charleston."

"Oh, how lovely," Laura cooed sarcastically. "Miss Charleston, the banking heiress, no doubt?"

"True, she was the eldest daughter of that particular family."

"I remember them."

Eloise stepped forward, frowning slightly as she caught something in Patrick's tone.

"Ye said 'was'," she offered timidly. Her father raised his head and looked at her.

"Sorry?"

"Ye said ye *were* married. What became of 'er?"

Patrick stared at her sadly.

"You're as clever as your mother," he said kindly. "She passed, I'm afraid."

Laura's smirk faded, a look of contrition replacing it.

"Do ye 'ave any children?" Eloise asked softly. Patrick shook his head, dropping his eyes, making it impossible for Eloise to read the expression therein.

"No," he replied. "It was the reason that Mary took her own life."

Everyone gasped in shock at the revelation, but Patrick was not finished, the shame spilling from his lips, unburdening himself as though he had been clinging to the terrible thoughts for far too long.

"I imagine that Mary always suspected I never truly loved her," he went on. "That my heart had always belonged to your mother, Eloise. It is difficult to compete with a ghost, a shadow, and she did try her best. God saw it fit not to put children in our household, despite us both wanting them very much."

His chin quivered slightly.

"He always knows better than us. It is always best to trust in Him and understand that there is a reason for the tragedies that befall us."

"I'm very sorry about yer wife, Mr Morris," Eloise told him sincerely. Patrick raised his head again and met her eyes, his own gleaming with unshed tears.

"You are a kind soul, Eloise. I am glad I have finally found you."

Eloise's chest tightened, flooding with a strange new emotion, one that she had not known before. Under the intense scrutiny of his stare, she understood that this man cared for her, without ever really knowing her.

"I will give you my name, Eloise, if Laura will allow it. You will want for nothing," Patrick promised.

"You can't make those promises, Patrick," Laura chided him. "Your father is still breathing, is he not?"

"Never mind him," Patrick said firmly, and Eloise believed him. "I am a wealthy man in my own right, with my own means. I make my own decisions now, Father be damned."

Laura's eyes lit up, interest tinging her cheeks with a healthy pink glow.

"What say you, Laura Miller? Will you finally do right by me, and marry me as God intended all along, so that our daughter will have my name and the life I can provide. I want nothing more than to get you out of this life of squalor once and for all."

Laura nodded, swallowing thickly, the tears she had held back finally slipping down her cheeks as they moved into one another's embrace. Embarrassed, Eloise lowered her head and ushered Thomas toward the hallway, closing the door behind her.

"We'll give them some privacy," she said nervously. "They've got some years te catch up on."

Thomas nodded but he did not smile, his expression diminishing the happiness from Eloise's face. She drew in a shaky breath, realising that she had her own explaining to do if she wanted to make things right with Thomas. She had not been fair to him when he had been nothing but kind to her from the first moment she had seen him.

"You could have told me who the Morris's were to you," Thomas informed her when they were together in the narrow hallway, their voices low so as to not rouse the attention of the neighbours.

"I was embarrassed," Eloise admitted. "I didn't want te admit that I was a bastard child without a father."

"You are more than your parentage, Eloise, just as I am more than my family," Thomas stated. Her blush deepened, humiliation growing. She thought of how she had mistaken him for his brother. How had it all become so complicated?

"We are each individuals of our own making," Thomas went on. "I believe that Patrick Morris is proof of that."

She gazed up at him and nodded slowly.

"However, I certainly understand why you felt the need to keep me at bay," Thomas continued. "If I believed I had been abandoned by my father as a boy, I am quite sure I would have a different take on the world at large. In fact, I believe you have held up quite well under the circumstances."

His absolving statement made her feel better and worse simultaneously.

"I shouldn't 'ave treated ye so poorly when ye've always tried te 'elp me," she told him. "I—"

"You have nothing to apologise for," he interjected, reaching for her hands. "In fact, I feel as though you and I have never really met on an honest level before."

Conflicted, Eloise cocked her head, peering at him intently.

"How do ye mean?" she asked slowly.

"How do you do?" he asked, politely, pressing the back of her hand to his lips. "My name is Thomas Warren Winslow—the first, I believe."

Giggling lightly, Eloise bowed her head.

"How do ye do?" she replied shyly.

"And who might you be?"

"Truly?" she demanded, looking up again. Thomas nodded.

"Truly," he pressed. "Humour me, if you will."

"Miss Eloise Miller," she replied, sighing briefly.

"Or is it Morris?" Thomas raised an eyebrow and Eloise flushed, her head swivelling toward the closed door of their room.

"I don't know," she breathed.

"I suppose time will tell," Thomas said smoothly, pulling her closer, distracting her from her worried thoughts. "Whatever your name is, I find you most intriguing."

"Oh?"

"Indeed." He brushed a strand of hair out of her face, his eyes locking with hers, a smile touching his lips. "In fact, I have found you most interesting for quite some time, Miss Miller. I have been watching you, I should have you know. I hope you don't find that too forward of me."

Heat consumed Eloise but her blood reached boiling point when Thomas' lips found hers, brushing softly toward her mouth to steal her breath in its entirety.

Goosebumps tingled throughout her body, her feet rising to allow for her lips to press more tightly against his. When they parted, Eloise allowed her eyes to open, Thomas' smile causing her heart to beat erratically.

"I do hope that I will see you again, Miss Miller, or is it Morris," he said huskily. "Not only at Christmastime but during every season, several times a week."

Swallowing the lump of emotion in her throat, Eloise nodded.

"I would like that very much too, Mr Winslow."

"Please," he said with a laugh, "call me Thomas, or Tom. Too many people tend to confuse me with my brothers otherwise."

EPILOGUE

THREE YEARS LATER...

*E*loise peered at her reflection in the mirror one last time, ensuring that the pearl combs were in just the right place. She had been fussing with them for several minutes to get them perfect but one continued to slip out of the high, intricate twist of her hair.

"Would ye like 'elp, Ma'am?" Lydia, her maid, asked, hovering nervously nearby. The servant always seemed at a loss for things to do, as if the household were not big enough to occupy her time.

"I thought I told you to leave for the day," Eloise informed her sweetly. "Isn't your family waiting for you?"

"Yea, Ma'am, but it's Christmas Eve and surely ye 'ave tasks ye need done 'ere before I take my leave."

"I do not," Eloise reassured her. "And if I did, my mother and I are more than capable of tending to them. Please, Lydia, go home. I'll have the coachman drive you."

"Oh no, Ma'am! That's not necessary." The servant was aghast by the idea, but Eloise was equally troubled by the woman heading home by foot back to the East End.

"You'll not walk easily with the box of gifts we 'ave for your brothers and sisters," Eloise insisted. She blushed, hearing the dropped "h" of her words but if Lydia noticed it, she did not comment.

"Gifts, Ma'am? That's too much!"

"Hush now, Lydia. Come along. I'll find the driver and he'll help you with them."

She rose from the stool, forsaking the issue with the combs. There were much more pressing matters to attend to. Lydia was correct. It was Christmas Eve again and time for the celebrations to begin.

The hem of her ivory dress crinkled lightly as she led the way from the main bedroom onto the landing of the upper floor. All of the chandeliers had been lit, the flickering candles casting a beautiful glow over the stairwell and the hallway as they descended.

"Have you seen Tom?" she asked the servant. The woman shook her head.

"Shall I search for 'im, Ma'am?"

Eloise stifled a sigh.

"No, Lydia. You shall not. You shall get your box of food and gifts and go home to your family, as I said," she chided. "I will not tell you again."

"Yes, Ma'am. Thank ye, Ma'am."

Eloise offered her a warm smile. She was thankful she was able to employ some of the less fortunate women and men from her old neighbourhood, some of whom had become too old to work elsewhere. Theirs was not a huge property but it did require extra care—even if five servants were probably too many.

"Find the driver and have him show you home immediately," Eloise instructed. "And… Merry Christmas, Lydia."

"Merry Christmas, Ma'am." Lydia said bopping a curtsey.

Lydia moved to the kitchen and Eloise turned towards the front room where her mother sat before the fireplace, concentrating on a piece of elaborate embroidery. A beautiful Christmas tree sat shining brightly in the corner, alight with decorations, garlands of red and gold draped about it. Beneath its lush, emerald branches sat a nativity scene, encased by dozens of presents.

How many times in my youth did I imagine a sight such as this one? Eloise thought, the bittersweetness of it overwhelming her in the moment. There was a melancholy, surrounded by this wealth and good fortune, knowing that so many lived just as she had with her mother for so many years.

"Darling, what is it?" Laura asked, shattering her nostalgic reverie. Eloise turned her attention back toward her mother.

"Have you seen Thomas?" she asked, a note of worry touching her voice. "I seem to 'ave lost track of 'im." Laura glanced up from her piecework, her dark eyebrows knitting into a vee.

"I don't believe so," she replied. "I'm certain he's about somewhere."

Eloise studied her mother's face, a twinge of relief overcoming her as she noted the colour in Laura's cheeks. Since her marriage to Patrick Morris, her mysterious illness had been tended to and accounted for, never to resurface again. Yet Eloise could not help but worry that it might return as abruptly as it had come.

"I do wish you would stop looking at me like that," Laura said a little bluntly.

"Like what?"

"I will not drop dead on the spot."

"I never said you would."

"And why are you speaking like that?" Laura pressed.

"Like what?"

"You're dropping your 'h's again."

Heat shot up to paint Eloise's cheeks and she turned away abruptly.

"I must find Tommy," she mumbled, leaving her mother to her sewing.

"Ellie…"

She paused in the doorway, reluctant to look back.

"You have nothing to fear now, darling. All of our dreams have finally come true."

Eloise's shoulders relaxed and she offered her mother a soft smile.

"Indeed," she agreed. "I'll send for you when dinner is served."

Hurrying down the hall, she listened for voices but only silence met her ears as she ventured toward the study. Knocking on the door, her father called out for her to enter.

"Papa, have you seen Tommy?" she asked, worry puckering her brow. Patrick looked up from his desk, appreciation lighting his verdant eyes as they took in the sight of his only child.

"You are the picture of Christmas beauty, my dear," he told her, rising. "No, I haven't seen him."

She blushed at the compliment, but her concern grew.

"Forgive me. I must find him. I seem to have lost track of him."

"Do as you must, my love. I will see you at for our evening meal."

She moved towards the door and, as she did, the sound of giggles erupted just up ahead, filling her heart with relief.

"Tommy!" she called out, rushing towards the noise. Chubby legs toddled out from the servant's quarters, Tommy rushing forward in a darling suit, already filthy with cream and chocolate.

"What mess did you get into now, my boy?" Eloise laughed, moving to scoop him up. His pudgy arms extended, he ran towards his mother, babbling as he moved, but he tripped over his shiny, new shoes, surprise overtaking his face.

Strong arms reached out from a doorway, capturing the toddler's fall before Thomas Junior could hit the hard, wooden ground and he landed safely in his father's embrace.

"Perhaps you should not try running races just yet, young Tommy." Thomas chuckled, kissing the top of the boy's curly blond head before joining Eloise's side. Relieved that her son had not taken a tumble, Eloise smiled at her husband.

"I feared I'd lost you both in this house," Eloise teased.

"You say that far too often," Thomas replied. "As if this house is too large for the five of us. What will you say when there are seven or eight of us?"

Tingles shimmied down Eloise's spine at the thought of bringing more siblings into Tommy's life. She had been having the very same thoughts lately.

"Are you ready?" Thomas asked, eyeing her appreciatively. "You do seem quite overdressed for the occasion."

She blinked in confusion.

"I'm overdressed for Christmas Eve?" she asked uncertainly. "Since when?"

Thomas chuckled and shook his head, setting his small son down on the ground.

"Not for Christmas Eve, my dear. For what comes first. Don't tell me you've forgotten."

She continued to stare at him uncomprehendingly as Tommy began to toddle off down the hallway.

"Don't wander too far, my boy," Thomas called out to his young son, but Tommy had already waddled into the distance, away from his parents. Looping his arm through Eloise's Thomas guided her after the exploring one-year-old whom they quickly found in the hallway, sitting on his bottom in front of the front door.

"You see?" Thomas chortled joyfully. "Even Tommy knows where we're off to!"

Slowly, understanding crept into Eloise's heart as she stared at her husband in amusement.

"You don't mean…?"

"Of course," he laughed. "It's a Winslow family tradition after all. Jack, Edward, Daniel and all of their children will be there, along with my parents. Don't tell me you had forsaken Pringles Toy Shop."

Eloise laughed but the sound erupted as a sob, causing Tommy to look up from where he sat in alarm.

"What is it, my love?" Thomas asked worriedly. "Is it too much? Would you rather not go?"

Eloise shook her head vehemently.

"No! No, I want to go. Of course." She sniffled and raised her head to meet his eyes. "I-I just never knew the name of the toy shop until this very moment."

The amount of joy she felt over such a modicum of information seemed inappropriate, but Thomas appeared to share in her heartfelt appreciation.

"I wish I had known that," he informed her tenderly. "I would have told you sooner."

He cupped her face with his hands, drawing her in close.

"What do you say, Mrs Winslow? Shall we take our son on his first shopping trip at Pringles Toy Shop?"

Eloise threw her arms around his neck, kissing his lips sweetly.

"Yes," she agreed as they withdrew. "But only if I can buy something for you, as well."

"Only one toy," Thomas joked. "The rest comes on Christmas Day."

"No," Eloise corrected him sweetly. "The rest comes every day, by the way of God's gifts he has bestowed upon us all."

~*~*~

Thank you so much for reading my story.

If you enjoyed reading this book may I suggest that you might also like to read my recent release 'The Little Stone Angel' next which is available on Amazon for just £0.99 or free with Kindle Unlimited.

Click Here to Get Your Copy Today!

∼

Sample of First Chapter

Wavering moonlight ignited the stone angel, casting an eerie halo about his crown. Masoned curls, hallowed eyes, outstretched finger, promising paradise just beyond his reach. Behind him, a white-washed church loomed forebodingly, accenting the gleam of the statue in its foreground.

Jessica gawked, transfixed. She was sure she had never seen a sculpture quite this large and certainly not so close. She was eager to put her filthy fingers upon it, if only for a moment before Gareth took note of her waywardness. Her guardian did not understand Jessica's fascination with the angels, nor did he care for distractions. If he were to notice her straying from the task at hand, he would undoubtedly deliver swift justice and keep a steady eye upon her henceforth, ensuring that she would never again touch the stone faces she loved so much.

Yet the threat of Gareth's wrath did not sway the girl, the urge to feel the smooth marble betwixt her fingers unbearable. This angel called to her, summoning her forward with his hollow stare.

Toes pressing through the holes of her decrepit footwear, she rushed forward, crystalline eyes luminous in the midnight cemetery. She did not notice the sting of fresh cuts on her feet nor the flip-flap of worn leather slapping through the mud as she bustled forward. Jessica was grateful to have shoes at all, worn as they were. Erin had been forced to go barefooted after losing a boot in the Scotsman's courtyard on a jaunt earlier that week. Gareth refused to replace them, citing Erin's ungratefulness as reason but Jessica was sure he would change his mind soon. Erin was his favourite, after all.

The statue was almost within reach, Jessica stretching her own bony fingers to touch the idol as she neared. Had she minded her path, she would have foreseen the open grave before she was upon it—and ultimately in it. Her left foot tripped over an exposed root, the right following suit, plunging her downward, to Hell.

Scabbed knees accepted the brunt of her landing, the hem of her holed frock twisting over her legs and Jessica gasped, properly startled by her spill. After several silent seconds, she gleaned she was uninjured but that did little to placate her racing heart. Dark holes meant for corpses were no place for a girl of nine, even ones who pretended to be as fearless as Jessica, the girl with no surname.

But Jessica knew she was far from courageous, despite the face she put on for her urchin siblings and Gareth. Fear perpetually clung to her emaciated frame, thinly veiled and prepared to rear its ugly head at a moment's notice.

She tipped her tangled mop of dark hair back helplessly, searching upward for a means out. Once, her messy tresses had been a deep red with curls as springy as the stone angel's. It had been a long while since a bath had washed away the caked dirt that clung to her strands, permanently staining them brown, hiding the lice that roamed freely about her scalp.

Stars blinked mockingly as she fumbled for her bearings. Thin lips parted to call out but immediately, she clamped them closed. She could not risk her companions being found, trampling about the graveyard in search of a scrap or coin to trade or sell for a spot of bread.

I'll make do, she told herself bravely. *I just need to keep my wits. What would Gareth do if 'e were me?*

She did not remind herself that Gareth would never find himself in such a precarious situation. He was far too clever for such nonsense.

Vivid blue eyes searched the muddy prison for means of escape. Thankfully, the freshly dug grave was unoccupied, a small blessing that. For all the corpses she had seen in her young life, the sight and smell never quite became commonplace to Jessica's senses.

Small roots protruded through the dirt to offer a solution to her problem.

Scrambling to her feet, Jessica hooked a small hand against one of the twines, straining her aching legs toward freedom.

She had not eaten since the previous night, as was the norm. Gareth saved their meals for work well done but the lack of nourishment made Jessica's arms shaky.

I will do this! she thought with intense determination, but God had other plans for her.

The ground was far too slippery to abide her movements and before she had climbed halfway, her fingers weakened against the slick earth, sliding the girl back where she had begun.

A small whimper threatened to escape her mouth but Jessica managed to smother it as she tried again to elevate herself from the open grave. Once more, her efforts were thwarted, her frail limbs no match against nature's defences.

After the third attempt, she did not rise from where she had landed, crumbled in the corner. She willed herself to be calm, to ignore the hysteria creeping up inside her.

This is 'ow I meet God? In the throes of a crime?

Perhaps she would not meet God at all, she reasoned. There were far too many penances for her to pay and she was already halfway to Hell where she was in that moment.

Squeezing her eyes shut, she folded her hands tightly and prayed.

"Dear Lord, 'ave someone find me a'fore I drop dead in the grave meant for another. I beg yer forgiveness for all I've stolen and if Ye should take me tonight, let Erin find the bread I've 'idden so that she and Jake don't go 'ungry. Amen."

Peeking through one eye, she saw no one overhead and again tightened her eyelids, pulling a protective shroud around her.

They won't leave me. Gareth will see I'm not with the others.

Again, it was small consolation to the panicking child who could hear little from her dirt jail. For all she could glean, they had already taken what they could find and were making their way to the roofless house on Elm Street without her.

Minutes evaporated, Jessica's breaths escaping in short, uneven rasps. Time lost sense as the moon lowered in the sky. Tears burned behind her eyelids and she sniffled. Perhaps she would not die but be found by a groundskeeper in the morning where she would be shipped off to an orphanage, never to see her makeshift family again. To young Jessica, it was a fate worse than death.

For a fleeting second, the smell of lavender and rosewater touched her nostrils, a woman's voice singing wordlessly in her ears. Peace stole into her soul as the familiar dream encompassed her. She permitted herself a moment of fantasy, knowing that was precisely what it was, her imagination at work. It was the only means of comfort she could grasp in such a helpless situation.

"Stop your bloody snivelling!" The poke of the walking stick against her shoulder forced Jessica's eyes open, head dropping back to meet Gareth's irked expression. "You'll rouse attention with your mewling, you fool!"

A fusion of relief and concern gnarled inside her uneasy stomach. Gareth's low hiss was a hair of comfort but there would undoubtedly be reprimand later. Erin and Jake appeared at his side, their faces horrified to see the girl in the hole. Erin's sooty eyes widened, tousled black hair falling over her heart-shaped forehead as she strained to reach for Jessica with her bare hands.

"Are you hurt?" Erin cried, ignoring Gareth's deepening scowl.

"Hush your mouth, girl!" Gareth growled, tapping at Erin to sit back against the lip of the grave. He readjusted the stick in his hands, extending his arm for Jessica to reach the end. Grateful for the rescue, Jessica curled her fingers over the smooth wood and allowed Gareth to lift her out. He all but tossed her aside, untangling his beloved walking stick from her grasp. At once, Jake and Erin flanked the child, studying her mud-streaked face for evidence of injury.

Jessica eyed her guardian warily, flinching as he dug his stick back into the dirt to glower at her. Leaning forward on the knob, his hands piled upon each other, he spat to the side before running his tongue over crooked, yellowing teeth.

"Have you lost your senses, running headlong into a grave?" Gareth growled. "Is this your way of seeking attention?"

Jessica shook her head vehemently.

"I couldn't see!" Jessica protested. "I 'aven't been 'ere a'fore to know where I was stepping!"

"That's no excuse!"

"Ye cannot fault 'er for a misstep," Jake said jumping to Jessica's defence. "None of us know this cemetery. It could have 'appened to any of us, Pa."

Gareth's eyes became slits of anger, his brows creating a vee shape.

"You've eyes, haven't you?" Gareth was unmoved by Jake's lamentation, his massive form looming over the trio. In contrast to the moonlight, his russet brown hair appeared black, hints of white strands illuminated against the beams.

He opened his mouth to speak again but an untimely cough sprayed from his lips before he could muster another word. The rattling fit passed in seconds as the children waited with bated breath. When he had recomposed himself, Gareth leaned in closer to glare at Jessica with chilled blue eyes. "You're bloody lucky no one but me heard your weeping."

Jake stepped protectively closer to the smaller girl, his gangly body shadowing hers but disappeared against the backdrop of Gareth. At fifteen, he was the eldest of the urchin siblings, only by months in front of Erin, but years of living in harsh conditions made him appear much younger.

"Leave her be," Jake muttered, averting his eyes from Gareth's intense stare. He instead fixed his attention on Jessica. "Are ye 'urt?"

"It would serve her right if she were!" Gareth barked, face puckering more before Jessica could manage to shake her head.

"It wouldn't 'elp us none," Jake fired back. "We're already down a boy, right?"

Erin sighed and nodded in agreement.

"None of this would have happened if Liam were here," she mumbled sullenly. "He was like a cat in the dark."

Briefly, the children exchanged glances, the memory of their companion rushing pangs of longing through Jessica. Their exploits had been much weaker in Liam's absence.

Liam 'as found a "beautiful life," just as Gareth promised him. We mustn't fault him for that.

"Enough chatter!" Gareth thundered, sensing that he had lost their focus. "Off with the lot of you! Do what you've come to do if you deign to eat tonight!"

His voice reverberated through the cemetery and the children scrambled to obey his directive. Jessica had barely taken a step to the left, eyes desperately seeking any token that would not need to be dug from a rotting body.

"Oh!" Erin gasped. The younger girl reeled around, heart in her throat once more.

"What are you squawking about, girl?" Gareth rasped, another trembling cough erupting from his mouth. Erin rose an arm and pointed toward the church. They turned to follow her gaze.

In the time they had spent by the open grave, a lamp had been lit inside the previously somber church, the flicker of light radiating by the window.

"Someone's been there all along!" Erin breathed, her eyes wide. "They're watching us right now!"

"Stop gawking, fools! Run before you're caught!" Gareth snarled, rushing off with his cane in hand. He was a shockingly nimble man for one so large, long legs carrying him effortlessly across the damp grasses.

Jessica remained frozen in place, her body refusing to cooperate with her racing mind.

"Come along, Jessie."

Jake slipped a big hand into hers, yanking her toward the exit and onto the streets beyond. Jessica peered back over her shoulder toward Gareth who had fled in the opposite direction. Their guardian did not pause to ensure they had followed but Erin, who sat close on Gareth's heels, stopped to look for her street siblings.

"Don't fret about them now," Jake growled, pulling Jessica away. "The priest isn't apt to chase us all. We'll be long parted before anyone sees us."

He roused a valid point, but Jessica realised she was not concerned about being caught. Her thoughts were already on Elm Street and Gareth's temperament when they arrived.

Jake shared the same dark thoughts.

"I'm sure 'e won't let us eat tonight," Jake muttered, hurrying along with Jessica firmly in his grasp. She panted and ran, her holed shoes slowing her down against the sodden ground but Jake permitted no languidness.

"Come on, 'urry up, Jessie!" he snapped with Gareth's impatience. Yet he did not release her, his grip tightening as if he worried she might slip away through is fingers. Gareth had never held onto her like that.

"What do ye mean he won't feed us? It isn't our fault there was someone in the rectory," she huffed. Jake snorted, running his other hand through a tuft of grimy hair. Jessica imagined that his hair, like hers, had once been much lighter in colour.

"You've lived among us too long to be such a babe in the woods, Jessie," he grumbled. "Pa looks for any excuse not to share his food. Haven't ye figured that out by now?"

Jessica was aghast, a stab of disloyalty piercing her chest at Jake's unkind words. Gareth had saved them, protected them, kept them safe when no one else in the world had wanted them.

"Yes 'e will," she squeaked, her little breath rough as she struggled to oblige his long strides. "I know 'e'll feed us!"

Abruptly, Jake stopped, his dark eyes storming over. Gasping for breath, Jessica also stopped, thankful for the moment to rest. The church was still in view but the light was no longer visible from where they stood. No one ran after them, their fist waving, demanding they stay put. They were out of harm's way—for the moment.

Jessica's frame still trembled from the tumble she had taken, her belly tight with hunger. She silently prayed that Jake's prophecy was wrong. She could not go another day without food.

"Did you take anything from the graveyard?" he demanded.

"I fell!" Jessica complained, her cheeks tinging crimson.

"Before you fell?" he growled. There was a modicum of hope in his dark eyes, and she loathed to diminish it. Jessica swallowed and stared up solemnly, shaking her head.

"No…"

Jake grimaced.

"Nor did we," Jake spat, again snatching her back toward the wrought-iron fence, any semblance of faith evaporating from his face. "I'm telling you, 'e won't feed us."

Jessica fell silent, her little feet rushing to keep pace with Jake. A rumble of thunder in the distance spoke of impending rain. She wondered if she should tell Jake of her secret end of bread, hidden amongst the tattered blanket she used to sleep. Jessica had found it in a rubbish pile, half green with decay on the very same night that Erin had lost her boot.

"We won't starve," Jessica piped up, hoping to alleviate his sour expression. "I've some bread if Pa doesn't give us supper tonight."

Jake scoffed but cast her a sidelong look of affection.

"I do!" Jessica promised. "It's 'idden in me spot!"

"Then it won't be there anymore." Jake sighed, squeezing her fingers gently. "The rats 'ave surely 'ad it, stupid."

Disappointment clutched Jessica's heart as she recognised the truth to Jake's words.

I know 'e'll feed us, she insisted optimistically but as fat droplets of rain began to pelt from the sky, Jessica could not shake the sense that God was telling her otherwise. It was bound to be a long and terrible night.

~*~*~

This wonderful Victorian Romance story — 'The Little Stone Angel' — is available on Amazon for just £0.99 or *FREE* with Kindle Unlimited simply by clicking on the link below.

Click Here to Get Your Copy of 'The Little Stone Angel' - Today!

A NOTE FROM THE AUTHOR

Dear Reader,

Thank you so much for choosing and reading my story — I sincerely hope it lived up to your expectations and that you enjoyed it as much as I loved writing about the Victorian era.

This age was a time of great industrial expansion with new inventions and advancements.

However, it is true to say that there was a distinct disparity amongst the population at that time — one that I like to emphasise, allowing the characters in my stories to have the chance to grow and change their lives for the better.

Best Wishes
Ella Cornish

∾

Newsletter

If you love reading Victorian Romance stories…

Simply sign up here and get your FREE copy of The Orphan's Despair

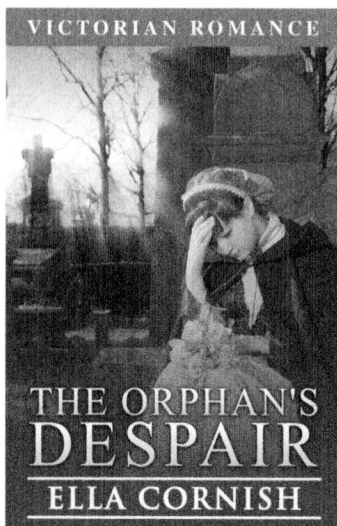

VICTORIAN ROMANCE

THE ORPHAN'S
DESPAIR
ELLA CORNISH

Click Here to Download Your Copy - Today!

❧

More Stories from Ella!

If you enjoyed reading this story you can find more great reads from Ella on Amazon...

Click Here for More Stories from Ella Cornish

❧

Contact Me

If you'd simply like to drop us a line you can contact us at **ellacornishauthor@gmail.com**

You can also connect with me on my Facebook Page **https://www.facebook.com/ellacornishauthor/**

I will always let you know about new releases on my Facebook page, so it is worth liking that if you get the chance.

LIKE Ella's Facebook Page ***HERE***

I welcome your thoughts and would love to hear from you!

Printed in Great Britain
by Amazon